A CHANGE
OF PLANS

A WHAT HAPPENS IN **VEGAS** STORY

ROBYN THOMAS

Entangled Publishing, LLC
2614 South Timberline Road
Suite 109
Fort Collins, CO 80525
Visit our website at www.entangledpublishing.com.

Lovestruck is an imprint of Entangled Publishing, LLC.

Edited by Alethea Spiridon Hopson
Cover design by Heather Howland
Cover art from iStock

Manufactured in the United States of America

First Edition June 2015

To Bernie, Matt and Rosie. "Birthday week" wouldn't be the same if I couldn't share it with all of you.

Chapter One

Bright lights. Big city. Anonymity and a chance to be recklessly, drunkenly single.

The mantra had fueled seven hours of nonstop driving, but the lights of Vegas made the words jumble in Sara's throat. Pawning her big ass diamond ring and living large on the proceeds had seemed like a brave move this morning. Now? Not so much.

Sara coasted to a halt on the shoulder of the road and scowled at the indent her engagement ring had made on her finger. Considering the size of the rock and the *years* she'd worn it, she should be glad the damage was so slight. She adjusted the angle of the rearview mirror and stared at her reflection, surprised to see the same old Sara returning her gaze. Perhaps she'd been wrong to come here. Maybe…

"Don't even think about driving back to Pity City, Utah," she told the woman in the mirror. "Leaving was the hard part. Getting rid of the damn ring and booking a room ought to be easy." Her eyes narrowed on the long brown braid trailing over her shoulder. "If you need some incentive, get a haircut."

The idea held definite appeal. Her waist length locks were her best feature, but they were what her ex had loved most about her. He'd actually told her that midway through dumping her, each new compliment like a knife to her heart. "You're sweet and loyal and you have pretty hair that never changes," he'd said in a gentle tone. "But honestly, Sara, I could describe the poodle next door the same way. You can't blame me for not wanting to marry a woman with no sense of style or adventure."

Actually, I can. I can also get a radical haircut anytime I want. With a decisive nod, she flipped on the turn signal and joined the traffic headed for Vegas.

When the six o'clock news came on the radio she began to panic. She was pretty sure you could drink, dance, and gamble all night in Vegas, but what hours did pawnshops keep? Nine to five? She hoped not. A burger might be affordable with what was in her wallet; a bed for the night wasn't.

She blinked at the sight of a strange white building adorned in striped poles with huge gold, red, green, and purple ribbons cascading down the sides. The Masquerade Hotel was disgustingly cheerful and kitsch. Staying there was bound to cheer her up.

She drove along the Strip, scanning the neon for the keywords "buy" and "sell."

"Please be open. Please. Please. Please."

Avoiding pedestrians *and* looking for a pawnshop was proving difficult, so she found a parking garage then set out on foot. An hour later, dehydrated and discouraged, she glimpsed hope in the distance and dragged herself toward it.

The pawnshop's shabby exterior was almost enough to make her forget the whole idea. She stood on the sidewalk, twirling her braid like a skipping rope, debating whether to go inside and accept whatever pittance they offered, or sleep in her car and find a more reputable looking place tomorrow.

"You can't afford a decent meal," she muttered under her breath. "Take what you can get, and make it last until you get the wedding insurance payout."

She shoved the door open and stepped inside, her resolve wavering as she realized that other patrons were browsing in the shop. It would be mortifying to have an audience while she bargained for funds. Everyone within earshot would know about her failed engagement. They might even think *she'd* called it off and kept the ring.

"Can I help you, miss?"

"Uh?" *No. Maybe? I'm not sure.* When the bell on the door rang again, signifying more customers, Sara plucked the ring out of her wallet and thrust it at the wizened old woman behind the counter. "I want to pawn this."

The woman bounced the ring lightly on her palm. "It's heavy." She gave Sara's peasant blouse and baggy harem pants a disapproving once over. "Did you steal it?"

"Of course, but it was too easy. No thrill, you know? It has quite a distinctive setting, so I flashed it around, hoping someone would recognize it. No one did." She flipped her braid back over her shoulder and raised her chin. "Now I've chosen a public place to try to convince a cynic to buy it."

A snort of laughter from one of the other patrons made her flush and stammer out an apology. "Sorry, that was rude of me." She dug in her bag for proof of purchase, shifting her weight from one foot to the other, wishing she could snatch the ring back and leave. "It's mine. I have a receipt from Tiffany and Co."

The shop owner tilted the ring to study the hallmark then whistled softly through the gap in her front teeth. "Tiffany." She seemed more interested now, but something felt a little off. Maybe it was too upmarket for this particular store?

"My expectations are low even though it's designer," Sara said. "I'll settle for f—"

She yelped in surprise when a man's arm encircled her shoulders and drew her against his side. He angled his muscular, suit-clad body slightly forward of hers, seeming to place himself between her and the shopkeeper, although he barely moved. "Darling," he drawled, "let the lady do her thing. She'll tell us what our ring is worth and *then* we'll accept or decline her offer."

Darling? Sara's heart beat a rapid staccato as Mr. Tall, Dark, and Possessive took control. Her gaze zeroed in on his chin dimple and refused to budge. The ridiculous urge to touch it, to trace the dip with her fingertips, made her freeze in place. Initiating contact of any sort was out of the question. She didn't even know this man. She couldn't fathom why he was pretending they were a couple, but his subtly aggressive body language suggested it was for her benefit. The air vibrated with tension as he and the storeowner exchanged hard looks. What the hell was going on? Why did she feel as if the two of them might arm wrestle?

"Darling?" Strong fingers prodded her shoulder, demanding a response.

Sara gave it without thinking. "We're happy to wait

while you value it," she told the storeowner.

When the woman turned away, and the man released his hold on her, Sara finally remembered to breathe. It was a mistake. The action lifted her breasts just enough to press against the curve of his elbow. She gasped and accidentally nudged him again, blushing when he looked down. Every other man she knew would have stepped back. He didn't. And she dared not breathe because he was still staring at the slight gap between her chest and his elbow.

She cleared her throat. "Why did you say it's *our* ring?"

His focus shifted to her face. A devastating smile curved his full lips, and then he laughed. "You needed an ally. I had to improvise." His amusement faded as he continued to look at her. "First time in a pawn shop? First time in Vegas? I can't place your accent. Where are you from?" He curled his hand behind her neck and brought her braid forward, nodding in satisfaction, almost as if he knew she preferred it there. "Tell me what you're doing here. You hopped a bus from—?"

"I drove." She took a step back and drew herself up to her full height. "From Utah."

"Why?"

She wrapped her fingers around her braid and squeezed, taking out her frustration on it instead of him. "I just—had to. I hate being pitied." His scowl told her she was in no danger of being pitied by him. After the week she'd had, it was liberating to interact with someone who wasn't affected by her broken engagement. "Saturday was supposed to be my wedding day," she said. "It's kind of a big deal because I've been planning it for twenty years." She ignored the way his brows hiked. "And everyone in my hometown is involved in one way or another. When Gabe called it off they started to smother me with attention—calling, stopping by for coffee, leaving casseroles and flowers and notes of condolence on my doorstep." She exhaled unsteadily, shifting her attention to a display case full of vintage hair combs. "One of my neighbors, a lovely man in his seventies, proposed yesterday."

He made a choked sound. "Congratulations."

"It's not funny. His proposal is the fourth one I've had this week." She tried to ignore his quick, doubtful appraisal. "It's not me they want." She worried her lip, and then shrugged. "I hadn't realized how excited everyone was to see all the wedding preparations finally come together. Apparently they don't care who stands up at the front as long as it goes ahead."

He laughed, and her tension eased for the first time in a week. She smiled up at him. "I took delivery of my wedding cake early this morning, and then my mailman delivered two hundred personalized bottles of champagne with heart shaped chocolates draped around their necks."

His dark blue eyes glinted with humor. "Did you smash them or drink the lot?"

"Neither. I put them in the shade on the porch along with a note that said *please take one,* and then I left." She paused. "Do you have a name?"

He leaned close and spoke in a hushed tone, as if his name was privileged information. "Ethan Munroe."

Being singled out by him was a heady feeling. She stared, waiting for him to add some kind of distinction: Ethan Munroe III, or perhaps Ethan Munroe, PhD, and felt confused when he didn't. The way he looked at her demanded…something, she just didn't know what. Her face warmed under his scrutiny. Man, he was intense. He could get a job as an interrogator of women. With a few disapproving looks, he'd make any female spill her secrets. She'd already told him most of hers, but he clearly wanted more information.

"Name?"

"I'm Sara." She hesitated. "Sara Greaves."

"May I?" He tugged on the receipt she'd pulled from her tote, and cursed when he read it. "The ring's worth seventy grand?"

She felt tears well in her eyes. Ethan's exact words had come out of her mouth four years earlier when her ex showed her the receipt. "Gabe took out a loan to buy it. He spent the exact amount on the ring that I'd saved toward the cost of our wedding. He said it was fair, that it made us equal partners going forward, and reflected his level of commitment." She shrugged. "Clearly, that was a lie. He refused to take the ring back though, so now it feels as if he's paid seventy grand to be free of me. Having it around gets me down. I just want to sell it quickly and try to forget."

Ethan frowned. "Sara," he said gently, "you need to ask for the ring back. If you still want to pawn it tomorrow, at a better place than this, I'll help you. But not here, not tonight."

I need money tonight. Our wedding costs blew out my savings and I had to tap into my business account. My credit cards are maxed out as well, and Gabe emptied our joint checking account.

The storeowner cleared her throat, cutting Sara's thoughts short. "It's genuine," the woman said. "You serious about parting with this?"

Ethan's jaw tightened. "One more day, Sara. What's the harm in waiting?" He laced his fingers through hers and tilted his head toward the door. "C'mon, I'll buy you dinner."

Sara almost nodded before common sense kicked in. Despite being almost too handsome and acting like her personal bodyguard, Ethan was a stranger who knew that her ring retailed for more than an average year's salary. Wandering off into the night with him wouldn't be her smartest moment. She gently disengaged her hand from his and stepped back. "Whether I choose to sell my ring or not, we won't be leaving together."

His slow smile caught her off guard. "Playing it safe? Good girl. Vegas must be a far cry from what you're used to, but you're a quick study." His voice was pitched low enough to keep their conversation private. "If you pawn your ring tonight, even for a paltry amount, it will be held securely until you redeem it with your ticket."

Money and safety and time to scope out the competition? You're a genius.

Ethan's smile widened as if she'd spoken her thoughts aloud. He settled his hand at the small of her back, his long fingers splayed wide as he guided her toward the counter. "While you're filling out the forms, wrap your head around the idea of eating with me once you're done."

Chapter Two

Vegas was Ethan's playground, his pick-me-up of choice, the one place guaranteed to infuse him with energy. But something was off on this trip. The familiar temptations didn't appeal. He'd been on the verge of leaving before he saw Sara vacillating outside a pawnshop. She was different. Intriguing. She had a braid that she turned like a skipping rope.

His assessment of her changed from minute to minute. It was damned infuriating. As a divorce attorney he often had to make snap judgments of character, and they were always decisive. Sara didn't fit into any of the pigeonholes he tried to slot her into. At first glance she'd seemed vulnerable, naïve, and in serious danger of being ripped off, but she was no pushover. His sweet little innocent had left the pawnshop with a dinner date, five grand in cash, and a check for thirty-two grand.

She wasn't beautiful or shallow, his favorite qualities in a woman, yet he'd insisted on buying her dinner. He didn't know why. Perhaps because Vegas was new and exciting to her? She had a bounce in her step, green eyes shining as she considered her next move. *When* she did something unexpectedly stupid, he wanted to be around. Vegas looked a lot better with her in it.

He tensed his arm, drawing her closer to his side as they passed a handful of drunken men in drag, one wearing a bridal veil. Even in their inebriated state, the men didn't leer at her. Their looks were appreciative, though, and he realized with a start that she was smiling at them.

Great. You're wary of a clean-cut guy in a Gucci suit, but you're happy to flirt with these morons. Why can't you pick a personality type and stick to it?

She sucked in a gasp of air, bouncing in excitement as she tugged him toward an all-night beauty salon. She stared, captivated by a giant black and white poster of a bald chick.

"Wow."

Her sense of awe tripped an alarm inside him. The poster was a basic studio shot of a model with flawless skin and too much eye makeup—nothing special, unless the artistry appealed to her. "Are you a photographer?"

"No, just an admirer. She's exquisite, even without hair, don't you think?" She trailed her fingers down her braid from collarbone to waist, as if running a silent comparison between herself and the poster. When she turned to face him, her smile was brilliant. "I want to go in. You're off the hook for dinner, unless you're willing to wait."

Was that hope in her voice? No way in hell was he leaving her here with a stack of cash. He gestured at the giant advertisement. "She's attractive because stylists have spent hours creating an illusion. Real women don't have that luxury." He sensed his mistake the moment Sara stiffened. "I know a thing or two about this, Sara. My mother—"

Sara finished his sentence, her words kinder than he would have chosen. "Your mother is meticulous about her appearance?"

He laughed. "You make it sound like a good thing."

"Says the man in Gucci loafers."

He plucked at his lapel. "My suit?"

"Also Gucci, although your shirt and tie aren't." She patted his arm and grinned. "I'm guessing the apple doesn't fall far?"

He stared at her, taking a moment to decide his next play. "If my mother was here, she'd lecture you." He winked then adopted a snooty tone. "When choosing a new look it's important to envisage how practical it will be at 7 a.m. on a weekday. Can you replicate it without assistance? How well will it be received in the office or fit in at the weekend farmers market?" He stopped teasing when Sara's face paled. He'd offended her. Again. Curving his hand around her waist, he guided her inside the salon. "Let's see what they recommend for you."

Ethan paced the sidewalk in front of the salon. He knew how long beauty treatments could take, but this was the first one he'd ever stressed over. Hair like Sara's would take years to grow, and seconds to destroy. He'd bribed the manager to give Sara the experience of a full makeover, without making any irreversible changes. As time passed, his faith in the manager dwindled.

A young woman in a fifties style floral dress poked her head out of the salon door, hot pink curls bouncing wildly. "Are you Ethan?"

He blinked at her makeup, wondering if she'd applied it in the dark. "Yeah."

"We want to dress Sara for dinner. Where are you taking her?" She sighed dramatically. "What's the dress code, darling?"

"Ah, there isn't one." He felt sick. Vegas had never held an ounce of stress for him before today. He'd come here ahead of his parents' upcoming divorce to soak up the atmosphere of greed and excess. Vegas was a city that supported his core belief: people only cared about themselves. Like his parents before him, he was self-serving to a degree that offended most people. Instead of apologizing, he embraced it. He lived alone, avoiding entanglements, aside from necessary ones within the work place. The freedom to always put himself first was worth the *sacrifice* of personal relationships.

He hadn't expected to have his views challenged by a wide-eyed country girl in hippie style clothing. Her opinions and behavior shouldn't matter, but somehow they did. He swiped his palm over his face and contemplated walking away. The only thing Vegas had to offer him tonight was inside the salon, though. He'd rather play tour guide than hit a bar or drive back to LA alone.

A vice-like grip on his upper arm snapped him back to reality. The woman with fairy floss hair led him inside the salon. "Come and sit down. How long since you ate?"

"I'm fine," he said, and then checked himself as he caught sight of Sara. He might never be fine again. The passably pretty woman he'd arrived with had been transformed into this stunning creature with bronzed, bee-stung lips, and legs worthy of a cheerleader. The simple halter neck dress had probably looked modest on the hanger, but it highlighted her curves as if it had been designed for her alone. Frothy layers of fabric swirled around her knees as she walked, sparkling beads danced over her breasts, and the delicate bow resting on her collarbone made it look as if the dress would slide off with one slight tug. His fingers itched to put it to the test. Her hair was loose and fell in soft, glossy waves that he felt compelled to bury his hands in. Long legs, amazing cleavage, a tiny waist, stunning hair, and plump lips just made for—

One of the stylists stage-whispered, but he was so deep in his contemplation of Sara that he didn't register the words. The reason her ex had put such an expensive bauble on her finger was suddenly clear. *This* woman warranted such a ridiculous gesture.

Sara stared at him, gulping in a breath that threatened to dislodge the top of her dress. His heart skipped and stuttered as her jubilant expression faded and her gaze slid away from his.

"Ready for dinner?" Was that gravelly sound actually his voice? Why was he blabbering about food instead of complimenting her? He found himself inches away from her and couldn't remember getting there. It was good, though; he needed to touch her. He reached for her hands, his thumb zeroing in on the indentation her engagement ring had left. "You look beautiful. Infinitely better than the bald chick on the poster."

Sara laughed in delight, her delicate fingers slipping between his as if holding his hand was second nature to her. "I'm starving. Please tell me we're going somewhere with decent sized meals and an obscenely late closing time."

He almost invited her up to his suite. Then reality kicked in. Food was what she wanted, what she thought he was offering. "The PepperMill never closes. If we're still there for breakfast, I'll be a happy man."

. . .

Sara pushed her empty plate aside and blushed for what felt like the hundredth time. She kept forgetting herself, staring at Ethan's jaw, wondering what it would be like to press her lips to the cleft in his chin. It was a good thing he liked to argue. Every time her mind started to wander he redirected her thoughts. He'd just reopened their marriage versus singledom debate. "You're wrong," she said. "I could prove it, but it would only embarrass you."

He smirked and gestured to a passing waitress for a coffee refill.

"Do you really want me to spell it out? You've never been married or engaged, and you profit from other people's misery. Being a divorce lawyer disqualifies you to argue *for* marriage because your livelihood depends on its dissolution. You bank on broken dreams."

Ethan raised his empty coffee cup and tilted it as if awarding her a point. "Nicely put, but perhaps I believe these disenchanted people deserve an advocate? I can't restore the happiness they once had, but I can ensure their property settlement gives them a fighting chance at another go-round."

Sara bit her lip then smiled weakly at their waitress when she arrived with a fresh pot of coffee. The debate-winning glass of champagne she'd planned to order no longer seemed appropriate. Ethan's career was the type she despised, yet he didn't appear to be heartless or mercenary. The way he told it, his clients were needy and turned to him for help.

"Would you like to see the dessert menu?"

Sara said yes at the same time Ethan said no. The waitress laughed and Sara amended her answer. "I don't need to see the menu. We'll have a banana split with two spoons, please."

Ethan swore so softly she couldn't be sure she'd heard him right. "That settles it," he said. "You may not know it, but you're already open to the idea of another relationship. It's only a matter of time until you meet a new man, fall for him, and plan another wedding."

Needing something to do with her hands, Sara reached for Ethan's coffee and took a sip of the black, sugarless brew. It should have steadied her, but all it did was make her head swim. "What makes you think that?"

His smile widened. "The ink's not even dry on the pawn ticket, yet you're having dinner with a man who's into you." He ignored her squeak of alarm, his gaze lingering on her mouth so long that *she* began to imagine him kissing her.

"Ethan?" *Stop looking at me like that. I'm going to pass out if I don't breathe soon.*

His gaze finally shifted, but the longing it generated intensified. Her lips seemed to have developed independent thought. They wanted to play over his. Could one glass of wine really lower her inhibitions that much? She'd better sit back and drink the rest of his coffee.

"I can understand adding an extra layer of polish to your look and dressing for Vegas," he said, "but letting hair like yours down gives a man all sorts of ideas."

"Hey—"

"But the biggest clue of all—"

The blood pounding through her head was so loud she couldn't hear him. Whatever he thought he saw, he was wrong. She would have told him that if the waitress hadn't shown up right then with their banana split. Ethan took charge of it, smiling as he accepted both spoons. He slid around the booth until the left side of his body warmed her right. He loaded a spoon with strawberry ice cream, her favorite, and then held it in front of her mouth. No pressure, just an offer of perfection for her to accept if she wished. Who could resist?

He reloaded the spoon several times, watching her with an indulgent expression as she ate from it. When he chose chocolate ice cream she shook her head and slipped her fingers around his wrist. "Uh-uh, that's for you."

Something dangerous sparked in his deep blue eyes, darkening his irises until they looked almost black. "That, right there, is the biggest clue of all. You cater for two. Every thought you have strikes a balance between your needs and someone else's." He focused on her lips again. "Mine."

My lips are yours? Liking the sound of that a little too much, she scrambled to come up with a reply. "I'm not thinking about you."

"Yes, you are," he said softly. "I've been on enough dates to recognize when one's wildly different." He must have felt her stiffen because his lips twitched. "It's a compliment, Sara. I can feel you taking cues from me. And there's an expectation I'll respond."

Good grief, the man was lethal. He seemed to know that staring at her mouth while talking about cues, expectations, and responsiveness would have this effect. Her earlier mantra repeated in her head. Surely, this was her chance to be recklessly, drunkenly single? Heart pounding, she leaned closer to Ethan and pressed a hasty kiss almost squarely on his lips.

He stilled, surprise etched on his features as he watched her. Then he moved, setting the spoon down and tugging loose the bow that held up her dress. He held both ends of fabric together, his dark blue eyes issuing a silent challenge. "Again."

She'd never been rewarded for bad behavior before. He didn't need to ask twice. She brushed her lips across his cleft chin, exploring the slight dip as if he'd invited her to do whatever she liked. When she snuck a glance at him, his features were relaxed and his eyes were closed. Her inhibitions melted away as she sank against his hard body and covered his lips with hers.

Chapter Three

Damn, Sara was sweet. She kissed like she was in junior high, yet he sensed that would change with the slightest encouragement from him. If he plunged his tongue between her lips she'd match him stroke for stroke, but it wouldn't be long before they were hauled into custody on indecent exposure charges. She'd probably expect a commitment after sharing a jail cell for the night. It might just be worth it.

He smiled against her mouth, knowing she wouldn't let it get out of hand. He opened his eyes so he could watch her realize what she was doing and draw away.

She pulled back slowly, a dazed expression clouding her flushed features. "I'm s—"

"Sara," he said. "I know." He re-tied her dress and pulled her to her feet before she had time to think. "Ready to see more of Vegas? What's your game: poker, blackjack, roulette?"

"I was planning to watch."

He grinned. "Plans change. We'll start with blackjack. Pick a casino. What's the first one that springs to mind?"

The wheels turning in her head were interesting to watch.

"Your choice, my choice," she said slowly. "I can't argue with that. Can we go to The Mirage?"

He nodded, expecting to be badgered with questions, but aside from insisting on paying for dinner, she didn't say a word. He slipped his arm around her shoulders and guided her outdoors and into a taxi. His tension ratcheted higher when she didn't seem to notice his fingertips playing over her upper arm. Back in the pawnshop she'd been hyper aware of him, and suspicious of his motives. Her sudden acceptance made him uncomfortable. If she'd acclimated to him already then he'd pegged her wrong right from the beginning. Mistakes like that were for amateurs. With the most important case of his career looming, he couldn't afford for his instincts to falter now.

He studied her as she stared out the taxi window, seeming to drink in the cosmopolitan atmosphere. She said something he didn't catch. Cupping her bare shoulder, he squeezed lightly. "Did you say something?"

She glanced at him then blushed. "Yeah, bright lights, big city. It's part of the mantra that got me here."

Why are you blushing? "Tell me the rest."

"Um?" She hesitated. "I don't remember. Something about being anonymous and single."

"And picking up a stranger for the night?" His smile widened when she didn't respond. "*Two* strangers?"

"No!" The color in her cheeks intensified and she tried to shield them from view. "I kind of promised myself I'd get drunk and act irresponsibly."

"Things you rarely do?" His breath hitched in his throat when her guileless green eyes met his.

"I kissed you."

That said it all. Kissing him so sweetly tonight was the only thing she'd ever done without weighing all of the pros and cons first. Holy crap, in his line of work he'd have sworn he'd encountered everything human nature had to offer, but Sara was a law unto herself. Sensing that his response mattered to her, he offered an easy smile. "Dating and gambling on the same night might be overkill for you," he said. "We'd better slow down and find a wholesome activity, something familiar and virtuous."

"Really?" Her excitement caught him off guard. "I know the perfect thing. I want you to take me to the tackiest wedding chapel you can find. We can sit back and watch people we don't know making the biggest decision of their lives on a whim." She tilted her head to one side and gnawed on her luscious lower lip. "You can predict which ones will become future clients. It'll be fun."

It sounded destructive. He could steer her toward a safer choice, but she *wanted* an ill-advised evening. She could have it if she agreed to hang with him for a few days. He had tickets to a ball at the Masquerade Hotel on Saturday night, the kind that would probably be a once in a lifetime event for her. He hadn't planned on going, but the promise of attending might be enough to keep her in Vegas. "Sure," he said. "Weddings tonight, gambling tomorrow, drinking the next day, and a masquerade ball on Saturday. What do you say, Sara? Do you want to extend your stay in Vegas until the weekend?"

Sara blinked. "No, I can't. I have to—"

"Lie to me if you need to, but be honest with yourself. Your schedule is free because you no longer have a wedding to prepare for." *Way to be sensitive, idiot. Skip to a safer topic.* "What about work? Anything pending? I might be able to get you a leave pass if partying will put your job in jeopardy."

"I work for myself," she said softly.

She didn't look like any entrepreneur he'd ever seen. "Doing what?" His voice had been sharper than he'd intended, but her answering smile was smug. Her attitude was strangely intoxicating. For such a gentle person she really knew how to hold her own against him.

"If you take me to a wedding chapel, I'll tell you."

He motioned for their driver to pull over. Fresh air would help if he and Sara were going to get into another debate. He wasn't accustomed to arguing with women. He usually dated the kind who sniffed out men with deep pockets then did their utmost to empty them. Sara was different. She didn't play by his rules. As if to emphasize that fact, she handed a bill to the taxi driver along with a smile and a cheery thank you.

Ethan's mental acrobatics as he climbed out of the cab were enough to cause a headache. Someone had jilted this woman? He'd never met anyone more suited to marriage. She had qualities that were categorically absent in *all* of his clients. A few hours ago he'd have said that marriage was the biggest scam and no one should enter into it. That was before he'd met Sara.

When she rubbed her arms, he slipped his jacket off and settled it over her shoulders, trying not to notice her little hum of contentment as it warmed her. He gestured toward the flashing signs of two different chapels. "Pick one, and then tell me what you do for a living."

She turned to assess the chapels. When she looked at him again, her gaze was direct and unwavering. "I'm a lingerie designer."

Inside his head he swore. The way she said it told him she was accustomed to defending her choice of career. Hell, what kind of people did she usually hang out with? "Do you"—*think before you say something offensive*—"have a label or do you specialize in one-off pieces?"

Her smile put the neon around them to shame. "I knew I liked you. You're the first man to ever simply accept what I do." She snuggled inside his jacket, making him wish he still wore it and she was cuddling up to him. "I prefer to work one on one and design a complete range of lingerie for a woman, often a bride, but I take on other projects when they appeal."

He swallowed, trying to ignore the multitude of images storming through his mind, not the least of which was Sara's own lingerie. It was lucky he'd had the foresight to cover her up before this conversation began. "Business must be good if you can afford to be choosy."

She laughed and started toward the closest chapel. "All that practice in the courtroom is paying off. Your ability to think one thing and say another is fascinating."

He didn't respond. Knowing when to keep quiet was another of his skills.

• • •

Sara's conscience rarely slacked off, but as she watched

Ethan pace the foyer of the chapel, his phone pressed against his ear, she realized she'd taken advantage of his company. He was clearly a busy man. She was certain he had better things to do on his mini break than babysit her. She tried to picture what he'd be doing if he hadn't met her, and blushed at the clarity of her imagination.

Ethan, naked on satin sheets, wasn't something she ought to be contemplating. She snapped her attention back to the couple exchanging vows. Would this become an anecdote for them, that crazy thing they once did in Vegas, or were they in it for the long haul? It was impossible to tell. They looked reasonably well matched, similar in age, both with bleached blonde hair and sun-kissed skin. Maybe they couldn't wait to get married? Maybe a big wedding would be ill-advised because their families didn't get along? Or maybe they didn't want to spend a lot of money celebrating a relationship that might not last?

She stared at the crescent shaped nail marks on the heel of her palm and forced her fingers to relax. Impeccably planned weddings didn't guarantee a happy future, either. She was walking proof. Yet she still wasn't sure where she'd gone wrong. Beauty and wealth weren't on her side, but Gabe had pursued her anyway. Her hair had drawn him in and her dreams had trapped him, he'd said.

Trapped? Had that been his exact word?

Making an effort not to inflict further damage with her nails, she curled her hands into fists. She hadn't trapped Gabe. He'd burst into her life and taken over, studying her future wedding plans as if they were a blueprint for happiness, then announcing that he'd play the male lead. She hadn't questioned him. In the four years she'd spent with him, she hadn't entertained a single doubt that they'd grow old together. She could have sworn he shared her certainty. So why was she suddenly single? And why was she torturing herself by watching strangers exchange vows?

"Leaving already?"

Ethan's question startled her, but only until she realized she'd left the chapel and made a beeline for the street exit. She paused with her hand on the door, sucked in a calming breath, and turned to face him.

"Yeah, I'm ready to go. Coming here was a bad idea, and I've taken up enough of your time." She gestured at the phone he was no longer talking into. "I didn't want to disturb you."

His gaze swept over her, hot and hasty. "You shouldn't have worn that dress."

She pulled his jacket closed, hiding the deep cleavage he was probably alluding to. "There are a lot of things I shouldn't have done today. Wearing a glamorous dress isn't one of them." She stepped to one side, drawing Ethan out of the doorway. A wildly intoxicated couple burst into the foyer. They looked unbelievably happy. For a moment she wished she could be carefree like them.

Will drinking help me feel that way? It's worth a try.

"Ethan?" She hesitated, wondering what he might read into a late night invitation.

Offer the man a nightcap already. How hard can it be?

"I need a drink. Is there any chance your hotel has a bar?"

Chapter Four

Ethan's instincts demanded he cut and run. He ignored them. Sara's eyes were guarded, her body language defensive, as if she was bracing herself for a rejection. All she wanted was a drink, and to escape this wedding factory. He wanted those things, too.

They weren't all he wanted, but Sara wasn't offering anything beyond a nightcap. Hell, when had a late night drink with a beautiful woman in Vegas gotten so complicated?

Sara's lips thinned. She nodded as if he'd just confirmed something. "You don't need the drama, I get it." Her anxious laughter tugged at him. "It was really nice to meet you, Ethan. I hope you enjoy the rest of your mini break." When she slipped his jacket off and held it out, he refused to take it. She draped it over his arm and turned away.

That was it? Not a chance. He waited until she took a step away from him before grasping her shoulders and spinning her around, pressing her back against the door. He crowded her, taking the kiss he'd resisted back at The PepperMill. Her hesitation, that delicious knife-edge moment of reluctance, was thrilling. He gentled his lips, coaxing her to join him, sensing passion beneath her panic. He eased his body back from hers, maintaining contact, yet reducing the intensity. It was the magic combination. Her mouth softened, opening for him as her arms wrapped around his waist. He groaned, wondering how much it was going to cost him to walk away from Sara tonight without asking for more.

He kissed her as long as he dared, watching as she touched a trembling hand to her lips afterward.

"If I leave you alone, you'll be married to some loser before the week is out. Don't argue," he said. "Looking like you do—like a troubled goddess—your plan is to hit a hotel bar alone and allow alcohol to dull your senses? You'll have vultures circling before you finish your first drink." He dragged his thumb across her lower lip. "You're so easy to read. They'll recognize your need for commitment, and if they're good, it will only be a few days before you wake up in an empty bed with a wedding ring on your finger."

Her delicate brows pulled together. "I'd have to be the only woman in the bar for anyone to even notice me. I wouldn't know what to do if someone did approach me, but I doubt I'd accept a sudden marriage proposal." She pushed against his chest, smiling wryly even as her fingertips tested the muscle beneath them. "I might avoid bars and get a room instead. I'll raid the mini bar in private."

He pulled her in for a hug, laughing softly against her neck. "And leave me to drink alone in a bar?" he asked. "Unsupervised? Vultures circling?"

Her tension didn't ease the way he'd hoped.

"I'm sure you'll be fine."

"One drink, Sara."

She hesitated and he could actually feel a blush firing up her skin. What was she thinking to warrant that level of embarrassment? "I'd like to, but I can't."

"You don't trust me?"

A barely audible whimper slipped through her lips. "I'm not sure I trust myself."

It'd be so easy to press for the drink. Hell, alcohol would be overkill. She was already in his arms. He could loop her hair around his wrist, kiss her senseless, and guide her to the nearest available hotel room before she had a moment to think. Temptation clawed at him. He rose above it. Again. "Let's get a soda at the Aria Café, and then you can book a room." He read both doubt and disappointment on her face when she eased away from him.

"A room?"

"A *single* room," he said. "I'm already a guest there." He stroked his knuckles from her temple to her jaw, torturing himself with her smooth perfection. "Tonight won't be the last time we see each other. You're meeting me for breakfast." He smiled. "And you're going to wear this dress."

Her eyes flashed a warning. "Like a walk of shame outfit?" She took a moment to think it over, seeming to warm to the idea. "I've already booked a hotel room," she said, lying. "It's at the Masquerade Hotel. I'll only do breakfast if you'll agree to show up without a jacket or tie, with your hair uncombed, your shirt untucked, and no socks. If I'm going to look put-together at the wrong end of the day, you can look as if you've just rolled out of bed."

He almost told her that would add to the illusion, but

the morning-after image in his head was too appealing to risk.

. . .

Sara rubbed her gritty eyes and groaned. She hadn't booked a wakeup call, but clearly Ethan intended to hold her to their breakfast arrangement. She didn't know why. Every time she tried to distance herself from him, give him the freedom to enjoy the mini break he'd planned, he started acting territorial.

She pushed her misgivings aside. If a hot, yet shallow, arrogant, successful divorce attorney wanted her company during his morning meal, then he could have it. She had nothing better to do. With no wedding to dominate her schedule, and no work commitments because of said wedding, her calendar was wide open.

Replicating last night's look proved difficult with limited cosmetics, and doubts began to creep in. She'd never broken a rule in her life. Why was she even contemplating walking around a strange hotel in a cocktail dress and heels, first thing in the morning?

The future you've always worked toward has vanished. You need to branch out and try new things. Reinvent yourself.

A sharp rap on her door dispelled her thoughts. She opened it for Ethan, and then froze. He looked like he'd just rolled out of bed, as requested, but she hadn't expected the intimacy of it. Her gaze swept from him to her rumpled bed, her eager mind tripping all over itself to pair the two. She forced herself to ignore the bed. Ethan, unshaven and deliciously rumpled, was enough of a problem on his own. In the four years she'd spent with Gabe, she'd never once seen him look like that.

Ethan swam in and out of focus, and she reached for the doorframe. His hand cupped her chin, helping to steady her.

"Ah," he said, "the effect I've always wanted to have." He leaned closer and lowered his voice. "What's up? Do you just need food or is it something else?"

"Gabe, my ex —" She bit her lip, fighting to stem the admission. "He never rolled his shirt sleeves up. Or left any buttons undone."

Ethan didn't move yet she felt him recoil. "He rose before you, showered, shaved, and dressed impeccably?"

She nodded, wondering how he knew the personal details of her former relationship.

"I'm familiar with the type." His words were bitter, and a thread of menace lurked within them. "I bet he folded his clothes over a valet stand before going to bed."

She nodded again, beginning to feel like a dashboard doll.

His focus shifted, his attention returning from wherever it had been to land heavily on her. "And you always felt like you were playing catch up, waking up stressed and rushing to pull yourself together? Feeling as if you didn't quite measure up?" When all she did was stare up at him, Ethan's lips twisted into a wry smile. "My father pulls that kind of shit, elevating himself by exploiting every tiny weakness in those around him."

Gabe exploited me? "I don't —"

She broke off when Ethan dropped his hand from her chin and gestured between them. "Today the tables have turned." He gestured for her to spin around, his soft growl of approval catching her by surprise. "You're the one who's flawless." He tilted his head toward the hall. "Shall we?"

Taking his arm and walking with him was easy, but her steps faltered when they passed a crowd of hotel guests all wearing plush toy hearts on their arms. She groaned. Hearts on their sleeves, really? The women were giggling, discussing the romance convention they were here for as if everyone in the world was aching to be part of it. They were wrong. This place was a nightmare for a jilted bride. They could keep their decorations and cheesy music. She'd get a room at Ethan's hotel instead.

"Chin up, keep walking," Ethan said quietly. "Vegas doesn't have a dress code, you don't know anybody, and just this once you don't care what anyone thinks."

Vegas doesn't have a dress code. I don't know anybody. I don't care what anyone thinks.

Ethan slanted an amused glance at her in the elevator. "You're chanting something in your head, aren't you?"

"Maybe."

"Are you having fun?"

Yeah. "Maybe."

"Rebel."

She laughed, forgetting her new mantra as she relaxed and began to look around her. Several people shared their elevator. No one seemed to care how she or Ethan was dressed, where they were going, or what they'd been up to. How long had it been since she'd felt so free? Back home every face she saw was familiar, everyone knew her business, and everything she did was relayed to Gabe.

For his approval?

The day she'd had a trial run of her wedding makeup,

Gabe called to instruct the makeup artist to stick to neutral colors. The one time she'd thought about getting temporary streaks in her hair, the stylist called Gabe to check his opinion. He said no, and she accepted his veto! No wonder she always felt unsure—she couldn't even apply a new lipstick without Gabe's say so. *He* decided when she looked okay, and she could count on one hand the number of times he'd ever complimented her.

Ethan's fingers stroked her upper arm. "You okay?"

No. "I need a new lipstick," she said. "A bright one."

"Before we eat?"

"Yeah, before we eat."

• • •

Ethan shoved his hands into his pockets and groaned. Casual distraction was what he needed this week, and Sara didn't qualify. Her reaction when she'd opened the door to him this morning plunged him back more years than he cared to remember. Had he forgotten the parade of women his father had brought through their house or had he just blocked it? How long had his parents actually lived apart? Was it just the one time, and why had his mother come back?

Heavy questions, and totally inappropriate at the present moment. He'd thought he was prepared to contest his parents' divorce, but maybe he was too close to be objective? His mother's answers to some of his questions had seemed a little off, but he hadn't expected her to lie to him. She'd said that she and his father had never lived apart. Now, with the clarity of his memories sharpening, he was sure they had.

Bloody Sara. Something about her made him want to

put himself in her place. Nothing wrong with that, except she kept tilting the View-Master and giving him glimpses of the world from her perspective. He didn't like it. Her sense of right and wrong was so simplistic it was childlike. Where were the degrees of blame, the levels of wrongness, the tradeoffs between one offence and another?

A hand waved in front of his eyes, and then her smiling mouth came into view. Her lips were plump, glossy, and outrageously *purple*. He wanted to kiss the lipstick off. Immediately.

"Now we can eat," she said.

He noticed her watching him closely, and bit back a grin. Apparently she'd expected the color to be an issue. "Statement lips," he murmured. "Nice."

Her confusion gave him the chance to sweep her toward the French patisserie he'd often glimpsed but never visited. Being with Sara gave him the freedom to indulge. She'd ordered an ice cream sundae the night before, so she wasn't the kind of woman who'd balk at a few extra calories. Her mind only ever seemed to narrow when she considered what other people might think about her.

He really needed to get back to LA to fine-tune his mother's defense, especially if she'd lied to him, but Sara's lure was stronger than the loose ends this morning's memory had unraveled. His parents' divorce was the highest profile case of his career, yet he *wanted* to let it slide for another day or two. For Sara. She was rocking five-inch heels and purple lips at nine in the morning because he'd told her she could pull the look off. No courtroom in the world could compete with that kind of power.

Chapter Five

Sara struggled to close her mouth and conceal her shock. "Your parents are getting divorced and you chose *a side*?" She lowered her voice, wondering if the waiting line at Jean Philippe Patisserie was the best place for this discussion. "How does that work? I don't even—"

Thankfully Ethan stopped her before she said something truly hideous about his lack of character and judgment.

"Our family dynamic is already screwed. My mother only turned to me for help with her divorce after my father chose to represent himself."

"I'm not sure if that makes it better or worse," she said. "I guess you didn't sit down to Thanksgiving dinner together."

He attempted nonchalance, and failed. "I don't think I've ever shared a meal with my parents. When I was young I ate in the kitchen with the housekeeper. When I was older I had my meals sent up to my room. Now I live alone and order in." He flashed a fake smile. "Holidays are for loving families. We've never been big on the whole turkey and presents thing."

"You'd probably hate the way I do it. I'm guessing hand-made bonbons and homemade plum pudding aren't your idea of necessities?" The momentary longing on his face made her wish she'd said something softer. Short of offering to spend the holidays with him, there wasn't a lot she could do.

Ethan's expression blanked into what she assumed was his "lawyer face." He seemed to regret opening up, and she was surprised to find herself feeling disappointed rather than slighted. It was liberating for someone to share their emotions without her feeling weighed down by them. Gabe had always held her accountable for the things he wasn't happy about, even if they'd occurred in the past.

She shook her thoughts aside and smiled at Ethan. "I kind of want an éclair, but if I order crepes I'll get to try the ice cream as well."

He rubbed his stubble with his open palm, his lips curving with amusement. "I was right," he said, as if to himself. "Meet me here for pastries at this same time tomorrow."

Slow, heavy warmth moved through her, making her toes curl. She had plans that extended a full twenty-four hours. It was a far cry from the rest of her life, which had been sewn up as recently as last week, but scheduling anything was a step in the right direction. "Tomorrow," she murmured.

"Stay for three days. You haven't gambled yet, and we need to go dancing."

She opened her mouth to point out the flaws in his plan, and found herself agreeing instead. "You're on—if you let me buy you breakfast."

They'd reached the front of the line, so he couldn't reply. He scowled though, and gave his order through gritted teeth. She almost laughed when he flipped his credit card out of his wallet at such speed that he dropped it.

"Smooth." Teasing him had seemed harmless while he was crouched near her feet, but she had to stifle a squeal when his hand encircled her ankle. Apparently, despite the outrageous line of customers, he'd found time to retaliate.

His hand remained in place long enough for his thumb to sweep back and forth in an arc, and then he stood. Without even looking he slid his credit card to the server, then he leaned down to speak in Sara's ear. "Deliciously smooth."

My leg? Holy crap, there had to be at least fifty people in the café yet Ethan had just…

He chuckled. "Breathe. Relax. You look a little stunned, but I assure you no one knows why."

Sara swallowed then gulped in some air. Ethan was right. She was practically having an out-of-body experience, feeling flushed and conspicuous, teetering on skyscraper heels, but the people around them were oblivious.

"How long has it been?"

Since I overreacted to a man's hand on my ankle? Oh, sex. "Ah, two months, almost three. The weekend before Halloween."

"He's seeing someone else."

"Gabe? No, he's just been busy."

"Too busy to sleep with his beautiful, lingerie-designing fiancée?" He gave her a hard look. "Did you live together?"

All the air left her lungs. She couldn't have this discussion *here.* Or anywhere with him. She shouldn't have to. His jaw tightened, giving her some idea of how intimidating he must be in the courtroom.

"Yeah, we lived together, but when your dream wedding is approaching and you both want every detail to be perfect, you accept that it will take over your lives. We hardly had time to eat or shower."

Ethan's eyes dared her to set the pretty version of her story aside and spill the real dirt, except there wasn't any. Gabe had simply changed his mind.

"How did he propose?"

She blinked at the unexpected question. "Um, video. He went through my dream wedding file and picked out the things he liked, and then he had friends and neighbors film him with similar items or at the locations I'd chosen. It was an amazing preview of our wedding day, and almost everyone we knew was in the video. He went to so much trouble. I couldn't have asked for anything better."

Ethan was silent for so long she began to worry. He didn't know Gabe, and he barely knew her; it shouldn't matter what he thought.

They collected their food and found a vacant table without exchanging another word. When Ethan cut into his crepe her patience snapped.

"Why have you stopped analyzing my ex?"

"I don't want to put you off your breakfast."

That bad, huh? She briefly considered arguing before deciding she'd rather eat than know. The forkful of crepe and moist, juicy raspberries never made it to her mouth. "You could be wrong. Gabe's always been somewhat restrained. I think it's because I'm not exactly—"

"Gorgeous? A lingerie designer? The kind of woman who'd melt into a puddle of need in a queue at an upscale bakery?" He made a low growling sound when she opened her mouth to protest his summary. "You said your whole town was involved in your wedding preparations. It's my guess that being the groom in such a big production" —he smirked when she rolled her eyes— "gave him a sense of distinction. It sounds as if the wedding was where your lives were headed."

She nodded slowly.

"But as it drew closer, he started to wonder if he wanted what would come afterwards?"

Damn, that fit surprisingly well with Gabe's recent behavior. He'd stopped wanting to talk about when they'd start a family, renovate their house, and update their cars, yet he was all about their wedding. She'd seen how obsessed he was, but that was only because he was supportive of her dreams, right? She racked her brain for clues that he'd ever been interested in her outside of their wedding plans. She drew a blank. Their first official date had been *after* a dinner party where her girlfriends had dragged her wedding file out and made fun of it. Man, why hadn't she put that together at the time?

"Sara?"

Aware that her hands were shaking, she set her fork down carefully and stared at her uneaten food. *Make an excuse and leave.* "I need to get my car." She got to her feet, white knuckles gripping the back of the chair. "Excuse me."

It wasn't until she'd hit the pavement outside the hotel that she realized she didn't know where to go. Nothing was familiar. Her car was in a garage…somewhere. Her fingers closed automatically around something that was pressed into her hand. It was a stupid move, but it turned out to be a white monogrammed handkerchief with the initials EM.

"It's clean."

Ethan. I should've known he'd follow me.

"Blot your lips then take a couple of deep breaths. We'll get you a comfortable pair of flats." His eyes made a lightning head-to-toe assessment. "And maybe a jacket. Then you can give the lecture on tact and boundaries that you're dying to launch into."

Her lips quirked but she hid the movement behind the handkerchief. "Remind me why I'd want to shop with you?"

"You don't." He slipped his hand into hers and led her toward the shopping plaza adjacent to the hotel. "What you *do* want is a pared down outfit more appropriate for day-wear. And you probably want to braid your hair."

Smacking him one was looking better by the moment. How did he know all this stuff? "What *you* want to do is practice being quiet," she said. "The last thing I need right now is a glitzy shopping trip. I'm going back upstairs to put on yesterday's travelling clothes and then I'm going to spend the day alone." She hesitated. "What you said back there—"

"Was wrong."

Or so damn accurate you should get an award. "I need a chance to process it properly before I decide one way or the other."

A weird sense of energy lurked beneath his calm exterior. She had the feeling he'd follow her unless she gave him a better alternative.

"If you're free for dinner at six, call the concierge for my room number. We'll make a plan."

• • •

Sara moaned in contentment as the massage therapist worked the last remaining knot out of her back. Last night over bowls of pasta, her comfort food of choice, Ethan quizzed her on what things her schedule would have held if her wedding went ahead. Then the bastard excused himself for a moment, returning with a smug smile and a booking for a comprehensive spa package. Not for himself, for her. She should've been too upset with him to keep the appointment, yet here she was.

"Keeping to your schedule wherever possible will help you," he'd said.

"Is that what you're doing? Maintaining your usual nine to five grind in the lead up to your parents' divorce?"

"Sara." His voice was weighted with frustration. "Vegas is my home away from home. I live alone, so when I'm not working, I bore easily."

"That's what hobbies are for. If yours don't hold your attention, they might not be the right ones."

"I collect vintage surfboards." His quiet admission was the last thing she'd expected. "Surfing at dawn is one of my favorite things, but I run into trouble when I try to fill the rest of the day."

She tuned back in to her surroundings as the background music changed from light classical to nature sounds. Distant thunder and steadily falling rain were the perfect accompaniment to her lazy day of pampering.

Sending her here had been a good call, but she'd spent most of last night trying to discredit Ethan's theories about her and Gabe's relationship. Oddly, his parting words were the most troubling.

"Enjoy the practice run at the spa, Sara. Next time you indulge in a full day of treatments you'll have a shiny new ring on your left hand."

He'd sounded so confident. Did she really seem like the kind of woman who'd fall for the same mean trick twice? Pinning her hopes on a perfect man, a fairytale wedding, and a long and happy marriage had never seemed childish, until now. Maybe the combination was universally appealing, the stuff of legends, because it was unattainable? Nobody was perfect. Even the most sensational parties ended. And if happy marriages were commonplace, Ethan's profession wouldn't exist.

"Try to relax," the therapist said. "Your man is planning a big night. Trust me, he's stressed enough for both of you."

Ethan was stressed? Over her? That was funny. She let her eyes drift closed and her thoughts scatter. Forever had passed since she'd had a worry-free day. If this was her chance, she'd be a fool to waste it.

"Time to wake up, sweetie."

Sweetie? Sara's eyes popped open and memory flooded back. She lifted her head and smiled sheepishly. "Sleeping is the highest compliment, right?"

The therapist laughed. "From you? Yes. You were wound pretty tight when you first arrived. When you're ready, get up and put the robe on. There are clothes waiting for you in the next room, but you'll want to apply your makeup before you dress."

Had Ethan had the foresight to arrange for her suitcase to be brought down from her room? That was good, although her clothes were all casual. "Wait," she squeaked. "Am I doing my own makeup?"

The woman paused with her hand on the door. "We have strict instructions not to interfere."

Sara stared after her, wondering if Ethan had any idea what to expect. He'd seen her without any polish the other night at the pawnshop, but she'd had a massive upgrade prior to dinner. There was only so much she could do tonight with concealer, lipstick, and mascara.

Oh, who cared? If standard Sara didn't meet with his approval, he could eat solo.

She applied light makeup, and then stepped into the locker room next door. She gasped at the sight of a bejeweled masquerade mask and two beautiful, silvery dresses. Both were long, one with a flowing skirt and the other with a narrow silhouette, one made of chiffon and the other of velvet. How could she possibly choose? And how freaky was it that he'd chosen silver, her favorite color, the one that would've tied all the elements of her wedding together?

A small envelope attached to one of the hangers drew her closer. She ripped it open. Apparently Ethan had anticipated her dilemma. She read most of the note before her limp fingers dropped it. The text landed upright so she didn't bother retrieving it from the floor—where it belonged.

Sara, I trust you're enjoying your non-wedding preparations. The outline you gave of your engagement calendar was detailed enough for me to set an impromptu agenda. Last night was supposed to have been your bachelorette party, followed by your rehearsal dinner tonight. We'll swap the order of those events, starting with a decadent degustation dinner this evening, and then a night of gambling, drinking, and dancing tomorrow. Dress for fine dining tonight, and save the dress you want to dance in for tomorrow evening. I have tickets to a ball at the Masquerade Hotel tomorrow night—hence the mask.

Your wedding has been rescheduled, *but you don't have to miss the all-important lead up to your big day, Ethan.*

She was so angry she could almost feel steam radiating from her body. The jerk was doing exactly what he'd accused Gabe of doing—getting caught up in the excitement of a well-planned event. She pulled on the faded jeans and threadbare T-shirt she'd arrived in, jamming her feet back into the spa slippers for added effect. This was the perfect outfit for staying in and ordering room service.

Vegas abounded with prospective brides. Ethan could search among them for another dinner date and dance partner.

Chapter Six

Sara didn't exit the spa as Ethan expected, but he wasn't disappointed. She looked fresh and clean, her glorious hair gathered into a loose ponytail that swayed as she walked. *Beautiful.* He stepped away from the potted Ficus where he was standing, utterly unprepared for the anger she directed his way.

"For a man who's so good at reading everyone else, you're pretty clueless about yourself."

Slender, ringless hands framed Sara's hips, subtly emphasizing their shape. "If you're so eager to get married that you're willing to ride the coattails of someone else's pre-wedding festivities, then for heaven's sake man up and get in the game. Hiding behind your profession, *pretending* you don't envy what your clients once had together, is beneath you."

She was wrong in every way that mattered, yet all he could think was *wow*. Gone was the sweetly vulnerable country girl he'd felt obliged to help. Here was a woman who knew her mind and wasn't afraid to speak it.

"I don't believe in marriage. Occasionally it works out, but I know myself well enough to recognize that I wouldn't fall within that small percentage." He fixed her with his most intimidating look. "You do."

She shook her head, her hands falling from her hips. "Not anymore." Her words were hard to hear over the crowd of people queuing for a nearby restaurant. "Good marriages are based on trust. That's something I may never do again."

He reached for her hand and led her toward a bar where a jazz band was setting up. She didn't ask why. The irony made him smile. On some level, she trusted him. When the bartender caught his eye, Ethan gestured at a drawing of the featured cocktail and held up two fingers. He steered Sara into a quiet corner booth, placing his hand over hers on the table to discourage her from giving him another piece of her mind. "Tell me you couldn't use a drink right now."

"I'd rather drink than go to a stuffy, overpriced restaurant," she said beneath her breath.

Amusement curled through him, a common occurrence when she was around. He allowed himself the luxury of wondering what kind of man she'd go for. People watching was a guilty pleasure of his. He often calculated the odds of a flirting couple leaving a bar together, a smarmy waiter getting a decent tip, or the time a seat would remain vacant beside a single woman. He'd never shared this activity before, but Sara didn't know that. If he sold it well enough, she'd think he was helping her. His tolerance for other people's company usually lasted a couple of hours, at most, and only if they were hot. Sara fit that bill, but she was also entertaining in a way he hadn't encountered before. He wanted more.

Their drinks arrived and he watched her return the bartender's practiced smile. Hm, apparently he wouldn't be able to cross smooth talking players off her future-husband wish list. Her taste ran toward the unexpected, but tonight could be an absolute scream if she loosened up and let him take his people-reading skills out for a test run on her behalf. He couldn't imagine what it would be like to look around and see only the best in everyone—nice, probably—but Sara was going to get screwed over again if she wasn't careful. He didn't want to see that happen. By the end of the night she'd have a far better idea of who to consider, and who to avoid, when she was ready to start dating again.

She took a cautious sip of her drink then screwed her face up and pushed the glass away. "It tastes like cough medicine, and not in a good way."

There's a good way? He assessed the shallow glass and estimated the volume at about five ounces. *How bad could it be?* Holding her gaze, he downed it in one swallow, and barely resisted the urge to splutter. "Ugh, what *is* that?"

Her laughter soothed him. He'd gladly drink a dozen more of the bitter concoction if they continued to amuse her.

"Wait here. I'll get something…else," she said with a grin.

She approached a different bartender, dazzling him with charm, if the improvement in the guy's posture was anything to go by. She performed some kind of charade to explain what she wanted, nodding several times when he held up items for her approval. Her focus remained on the bartender, but as Ethan scanned the surrounding area he saw that multiple gazes had followed her long ponytail all the way down to where it rested against her shapely backside. She bobbed her head, setting her ponytail in motion in a way that ought to be illegal. Holy God, what had possessed her to wear those jeans? The way they cupped her, accentuating her curves, made him want to stand behind her. To shield her from view, sure, but also to find out if she felt as good as she looked. If she leaned forward, rested her forearms on the bar... He shifted uncomfortably, struggling to bring his thoughts under control.

When she turned away from the bar, he saw what she'd bought, and burst out laughing. The glasses were shaped like a hula dancer's body. The drinks consisted of bright layers of red and yellow, and they were garnished with skewers of fresh fruit. She couldn't have chosen anything less appropriate for him if she'd tried.

He waited till she got close enough to hear him. "You bought me a Mai Tai?"

"Nope, it's a Tequila Sunrise. Don't knock it till you try it."

He accepted one of the glasses and touched its rim against hers with a satisfying click. "Last to finish buys the next round?" Before she could answer, he discarded the straw and garnish, and drank deeply. It was surprisingly good. He set the glass down and lounged back in his seat. He closed his eyes, savoring the sweetness, the tang, and the soft kick of alcohol. The tastes would forever be linked to Sara. He found himself contemplating a mass purchase of OJ, tequila, and whatever else lurked in his glass. He liked the idea of winding down each evening "with Sara" after he returned to LA.

Sara broke into his thoughts. "Looks like you're buying

the next round."

Her empty glass mocked him. Man that was quick. He studied her face, searching for signs of deception and finding none. "Can I buy you dinner instead?"

"Not if it has strings attached. If what you have in mind has anything to do with my wedding, fancy silver dresses, or you acting like a stand-in groom, you'd best leave now."

She was sexy when she stood up for herself. "I'm only offering food. Do you want it?"

She smirked. "I'll consider eating with you, after you've taught me to gamble." Her teeth closed gently around a chunk of pineapple then slid it off the skewer. She moaned ecstatically. "It's so good."

The carnal sound hit him like a freight train. Sara was in a bad place emotionally. She was off limits. Unless— "Time to go."

If his gruff order bothered her, she didn't show it. She waved her skewer at him.

"Soon. I've got to get my fruit fix. You need to finish what would have been my drink of choice if I'd made it to my bachelorette party."

Right. That. Her particular blend of innocence, sensuality, and backbone scrambled his brain, making him forget what their night was supposed to be about. It was time he got his head back in the game. Tomorrow, or Sunday at the latest, he'd have to head home. He didn't want to leave before Sara had a plan that extended beyond her proposed wedding date, so making tonight count was imperative.

Within seconds he'd slid the fruit off Sara's skewer onto a paper napkin, drained his glass, and stood up. "C'mon, even though we've missed our dinner reservation, we've got a schedule to keep."

. . .

Sara sipped her champagne refill as she watched Ethan win another hand of poker. She'd never played before, but being on "Team Ethan" made her feel involved. He was good at including her, she realized with a start. His attention always seemed to be partly on her. Even now, while concentration mattered, he flicked a glance at her, checking on her in a way Gabe never had. *For a man who didn't do relationships, he was awfully attentive.*

She set her glass of bubbles down, happy to blame the champagne for her sudden interest in Ethan. Despite his career and the situation with his parents, he didn't seem like the kind of person who'd have an inability to commit. She could understand him wanting to safeguard his assets, and his heart, but not at the expense of his future happiness. Didn't he want more from life than corporate success, the company of attractive, shallow women, and access to a surf beach at dawn?

She sipped her champagne as she tried to solve the Ethan puzzle. If he was so content with his life, then why was here in Vegas—with her?

His arm curved around her waist, startling her. The heat of his hand burned through her T-shirt, the lazy stroke of his fingers sending her pulse rate up. "That's the thing about learning," he said. "It doesn't mix well with daydreaming."

"Learning the rules would be pointless for me. I'm too easy to read."

"It's one of my favorite things about you."

He'd begun steering her toward the roulette tables, but she stopped walking, preferring to stand still while she argued with him.

"That's like me singling out arrogance as my favorite thing about you. It's part of you, but there'd be something seriously wrong if arrogance was your *best* quality."

"Sara." His jaw clenched, and she watched, fascinated, as he slowly relaxed. "I'm familiar with backhanded compliments. I assure you that wasn't one of them. Have you ever noticed that Barbie—"

"The doll?" What the hell? First he'd accused her of wearing her heart on her sleeve, and now he was comparing her to *Barbie?*

"Barbie is available with a *lot* of accessories, and presumably that's to encourage children to role-play. Yet, her expression is fixed into a forced smile. I've often thought that LA takes its cues from Barbie. Everyone chases perpetual youth while hiding behind a tan and a fake smile."

I'm different. The knowledge gave a whole new meaning to his earlier comments. She frowned at him, knowing it would make him smile. "I'd hate to go up against you in court. I'm starting to think you could talk your way out of anything."

He laughed and tilted his head toward the exit, starting to walk before she'd agreed to join him. "You might want to find a husband before you start planning your divorce."

"You might want to take your own advice."

"Ah, but I don't want a husband, or a wife. I just want dinner."

Actually, dinner sounded pretty good.

"Your silence implies agreement. You've acknowledged

that you might, one day, consider marrying." He smirked when she expelled a frustrated breath. "I tell you what. We'll do a sweep of the area while we eat, identifying hypothetical potential future husbands for you and comparing your impression of them with mine."

"Don't even joke about it. Keep your people-reading skills to yourself or find someone else to eat with."

"Steak and seafood?" he asked with such an air of innocence she had to laugh.

"Sure."

He'd all but promised not to matchmake, but as they meandered through the evening crowds she sensed him studying people and making silent assessments. She nudged him in the ribs as they passed a woman who looked like Barbie come to life.

"One of your friends?"

The tug he gave her ponytail was totally worth it. He pointed at the blonde's companion, who was built like a linebacker.

"Too tall for you?"

"Too *everything*," she said without thinking. "Imagine trying to feed someone like that."

Ethan chuckled. "Your two o'clock. Pinstripe suit."

Better. Less daunting.

"Do you *want* to eat alone?"

"Sooner or later you're going to have to decide whether or not to accept a date with someone. You'll need to think carefully, because if you accept, the guy will want another date, and another."

"You don't know that."

"Sara." He stopped walking and stared at her with an

intensity that stole her breath. "You're the reason people get married. You're the exception, the dream wife men hope to get, yet rarely do. The very next guy who recognizes that potential in you will want to *marry* you."

"You're the only one who's taking notice of me. No one else is debating my marital status or pushing me to grab the next available man and marry him. I'm not what you're used to, I get that, but I'm more than just a potential bride. If you can't think of me as a woman, then I don't think we should spend time together."

"You're very feminine. Trusting. Beautiful. And as fabulous as you'd look in a wedding gown, you'd look better out of it." His hand slid around the back of her neck and drew her ponytail forward, curling it around his wrist then allowing it to slowly unfurl and slide down her body. "I'd prefer to skip dinner and go upstairs."

"But—"

"It's not what you expected?" He stole her breath by repeating the slow wind up and release of her hair, the back of his hand playing over her chest. "I'm not expecting anything beyond gambling and dinner. Others will though, especially if they buy into your dreams. You've been on a crash course with commitment since you were five. If you want to avoid making another mistake, you need to be honest about what you want, what you need, and what's important to you. And you need to do it now, while you're single."

Chapter Seven

Sara's instincts screamed a host of contradictory instructions. *Run. Listen. Kiss him.* She spied the bar they'd been at earlier and headed for it on shaky legs. Adding alcohol to her current list of problems probably wasn't a good idea. But it beat trying to answer Ethan.

"One tequila sunrise," Ethan said to the bartender who'd served her before. "And a water."

Sara scowled at Ethan then hoisted herself onto a barstool and addressed the bartender. "Ignore him. Two please. And a double shot of whiskey on the rocks."

To his credit, Ethan stood quietly while their drinks were mixed. His silence and proximity ate at her, though, and the fact that he was standing rather than sitting finally tripped her patience. She gestured out the door of the bar in the general direction they'd come from.

"What was that about?" she asked. "Is this what you do to drum up future business? You trawl Vegas in your spare time looking for susceptible people, build them up until they think they can't lose, and then wait around for the bottom to fall out of their world? Is it fun for you to watch them risk everything, crash and burn, and then come crawling to you, the only divorce attorney they've ever met, begging for help?"

A warning flashed in his eyes. She was too wound up to heed it. She reached for the glasses the bartender set on the counter, grabbing both cocktails, because this was definitely a two-drink problem.

Ethan peeled a note out of his wallet and tossed it across the bar, his gaze resting on her the entire time.

"I'm being rude, I know. It's not exactly a 'perfect wife' kind of thing to do, but I never expected to have to defend my right to be ordinary." She glared at Ethan over the rim of her glass as she drank a good portion of the first cocktail. "I'm okay if all you see when you look at me is a small-town girl with a broken engagement and no college degree to fall back on. You're right. I bet everything and lost, and now I have to start over." The alcohol buzzed through her system, and she smiled wistfully. "I'm not deluding myself. I know I'm not glamorous or wealthy or well connected, but those things don't count for much outside of LA society."

"Are you done?" Ethan made an impatient sound and shook his head. "Drink up. If you get tipsy you might be easier to reason with."

Enjoying a double sunrise was the easiest choice she'd made in a long time. What wasn't to like about this moment—soft jazz playing, muted lights adding a surreal glow, *two* fabulous drinks at her disposal, and a silent, yet drool-worthy, man perched on the barstool beside her. She slowly stirred the last quarter of her second drink, torment-ing Ethan with the delay.

He picked up his glass and knocked the whiskey back as if it was water. "You overlooked the most obvious explana-tion," he said quietly.

"Which is?"

"I was serious back there. You're walking around assum-ing that you're *this…*" He slammed his ice filled glass down in front of her. "When really you have no idea." He nudged one of the cocktail glasses until it sat alongside his tumbler. "Guess which one you are?"

She hadn't thought him capable of earning another genuine smile from her, ever. She'd been wrong.

He growled long and low then reached out to stroke the center of her bottom lip. "And there's the crux of your problem. You're too quick to trust."

His tone, his touch, and his attitude confused her. She couldn't tell if he was praising or insulting her, and it was starting to matter.

"When you first met your ex, why did you go out with him? Don't think, just answer."

"He was a last minute guest at a dinner party I held for a friend's birthday. I hadn't met him before. He stayed behind to help with the dishes, and when he was leaving he sug-gested we get together again."

Ethan's brows dipped as if he was annoyed with her re-sponse. "And when did your elaborate wedding plans first come up? When did you mention you'd spent years planning the party of the century?"

She shifted on her seat, toying with her empty glass and avoiding Ethan's gaze.

"Tell me."

"My friends dragged my wedding file out and made fun of it, and me, the first night I met Gabe."

"Honesty," he murmured. "It's your defining characteristic. You're going to need it in your future partner." He lifted his fingers off the bar a little, a subtle signal that dissuaded her from commenting. "What else? Play the game with me, Sara. It's only hypothetical, just a bit of harmless barroom fun. If you could build your perfect future partner from the ground up, starting with honesty, what would your second ingredient be?"

She was tempted to shut his game down. Wishing for something didn't make it real, and setting her expectations too high would only lead to disappointment. Hell, she was *already* disappointed, and she'd gone into her last relationship without any hopes beyond a second date. If she'd known what to look for, which questions to ask, maybe she wouldn't have gotten in so deep. Aware that she'd been silent too long, she glanced at Ethan.

"I'd need him to be comfortable with what I do for a living." The slight tilt of his head encouraged her to elaborate. Her words came out in a rush, tumbling over each other in their haste to be heard. "Lingerie is delicate and feminine and beautiful. Sometimes it's blatantly sexy, but that distinction is generally bestowed upon it by a third party rather than the wearer. It *becomes* sexy when it hugs the right curves. The same could be said for evening gowns and sports cars."

His smile was slow and intimate, a silent invitation to lean closer and keep talking.

"There's nothing sordid about making ordinary women

feel like supermodels. I love the challenge of designing underwear that enhances a woman's view of herself and her body." She broke off, trying to ignore the sudden warmth in her cheeks as she realized how long she'd gone on. "Acceptance is important to me," she said softly.

He nodded, his gaze lingering on her before peering over her left shoulder. He seemed to be scanning the booths for a vacancy.

"Food?" she asked.

"Yeah. No more drinking for you tonight. There are better ways to spend your cancelled wedding day than driving the porcelain bus."

She stared at him, her mouth slack.

"You're probably due a hangover, but if you switch to water now, it won't be debilitating. Do you play golf?"

Golf? He'd stopped making sense. Just how much had she had to drink?

"No to golf, yes to food, but I want to get some air first."

• • •

Walking arm in arm with Sara along the Strip was an experience Ethan hadn't anticipated. She'd definitely overindulged because her non-stop chatter was punctuated with giggles, and she'd forgotten that she was wearing slippers. Seeing her this way, utterly relaxed on the eve of her non-wedding day, did him good. He'd come to Vegas looking for a diversion. He'd found it in her.

Her view of the world differed from his in every conceivable way. Aside from being in the same place at the same time, they had nothing in common. The kicker was that he hadn't been equipped to handle his parents' divorce until he'd met her. Representing his mother, going up against his father, had been fine in theory, but as their first court date drew near he'd felt it choking the life out of him. Vegas had beckoned, promising a reprieve from the overwhelming negativity of his daily life. He hadn't counted on meeting Sara. She was walking proof that marriage *could* work. She hadn't actually made it down the aisle, but when she did, no matter who she married, he was certain she'd make the union a resounding success.

"Ethan, you haven't heard a word I've said. Which means" —she bounced excitedly— "you owe me, and I get to choose where we eat."

He forced his gaze away from all the lovely bouncing, his mouth watering when he realized she'd chosen a pizzeria. At first it looked as if all the tables were taken, but Sara smiled at a middle-aged couple and asked to join them, taking a seat the moment they said yes. Ethan hesitated, unaccustomed to second-class arrangements of any kind. Why was she sitting? It shouldn't be hard to find another pizza place with free tables.

When the couple offered Sara the last of their bottle of wine, he thought his head might explode. No way had he just seen her nod. "*Sara.*"

She looked pointedly at the single remaining seat, smiling smugly when he dropped into it.

"This is Ethan," she told her new friends.

A harried looking waiter skated to a stop at their table, his expression bordering on contempt as he realized they'd seated themselves at a table he'd already served food to. Sara beamed at him.

"Hi." She glanced at Ethan. "Any allergies? Anything you don't want?" She grinned when he shook his head. "Too easy," she said. "One extra-large pizza with the works, two glasses of soda, and a bottle of that." She pointed to the wine on the table. "Thank you."

Ethan watched in amazement as the waiter scribbled down her request then departed with an easy smile.

"What brings you to Vegas?" their female companion asked. "Pete and I try to make it here a couple of times a year just to recharge our batteries. It's such good value, especially if you book in advance. We're here alone this trip, but we'll be back in three weeks to catch up with our son. Do you and Ethan have friends here? Have you caught any live shows? There's a great one—"

Pete covered his wife's hand and patted it gently. "Let Sara get a word in, Ellie."

"I'm going to let her talk." She added cream and sugar to her coffee in silence, although it was clear she wanted to pester Sara with further questions.

Ethan's gaze slid between Pete, Ellie, and Sara. The couple was obviously happy together and Sara had clicked with them on some unknown level. He felt like the odd man out, an unusual circumstance for him. Unease tiptoed up his spine as he realized his usual social banter wasn't going to cut it here.

He needn't have worried. Sara angled a sweet smile his way and answered for both of them. "My life kind of imploded last week and I had to get away. I bumped into Ethan not long after I arrived, and he's been kind enough to show me around."

It had been a long time since Ethan had been subjected

to the "parent look", but that didn't stop Ellie and Pete from giving it. Apparently they liked what they saw, and he wasn't sure whether to be relieved or offended. Eating mass produced pizza, late in the evening, in a raucous and crowded restaurant, under scrutiny from random strangers, was about as far as you could get from the elegant degustation dinner he'd booked earlier. It didn't begin to measure up, but this was Sara's choice.

He froze, his heart tripping erratically as he considered what eating here said about him. When had he adopted Sara's give and take approach to life? His word was usually law. He decided on the company he'd keep and the places they'd frequent. No exceptions.

When the waiter delivered their wine, Ethan reached for it, glad to have something to occupy his hands. He filled Sara's glass and watched her take a generous swallow, remembering too late that he'd told her to drink water for the rest of the night. Dammit, she hadn't listened, and his mind wasn't as clear as it should be either.

Splitting the bottle beat letting her drink the whole thing. His one job tonight was to make sure she didn't do anything she'd regret.

Chapter Eight

"That guy," Ethan said several hours and two bars later. "The quiet, studious one with the sweater vest and glasses."

A chill permeated the air around her. She rubbed her arms to ward it off. Ethan had been suggesting possible future husbands for her all night. His latest description fit her ex a little too well.

"Stop it. I'm never going to choose a man on looks alone. I'm not sure I want one at all, ever again."

Ethan spun her barstool toward him and eased her knees apart so he could step between them. He pushed her hands aside, his warm palms encircling her arms and slipping up and down. Her core body temperature catapulted from icy to overheated in the space of a few seconds. It was so easy to imagine those large, capable hands roaming all over her. How unfair was it that the only man who affected her was hell-bent on matching her with someone else?

"Enough." She reached for his hips, forcing herself

to push him away. "This whole 'what about him' game is pointless."

"It's not pointless. You decided what you wanted your life to look like when you were five years old. You don't even breathe until you're sure it won't affect your plans."

"My wedding plans?" Her tone was flat, lifeless. "You're right. I chose a man who wanted the same things I did." She snorted. "And together we put too much emphasis on a big, showy party."

"You did, but it's what was meant to come after the party that you can't live without. You've built a life for two people, Sara."

"Stop saying that. I planned a wedding for two people. It's not uncommon."

"Not the wedding," he said gently. "You're obviously great at planning events, but you thought well beyond your wedding day. You bought a house. You're self-employed with a good income and a flexible work schedule. If necessary, you could probably relocate without any drama."

His logic was damned annoying.

"You dreamed so big and in such detail that *any* man could step into your ex's shoes and make it work with you. Look around. If you chose a partner here tonight at random—any single, eligible man—I guarantee the two of you would be blissfully happy in a month's time."

"Any man?" She laughed to cover the hurt he'd inflicted. "The way you tell it I've spent my whole life constructing a cage to house some poor schmuck, and by month's end he'll know better than to say he's not happy living in there."

Ethan was silent for a long time. Exasperation poured off him. "How many unattached men, in an acceptable age range for you, do you think there are in this bar?"

"I don't know. Ten or twelve?"

He beckoned the bartender closer and ordered a dozen shots of tequila. He lined them up in two neat rows in front of Sara, glaring at her when she began to stand up. "I bet you'll be happy in thirty days if you get married tonight. You don't have to drink a single one of these. Just admit there's an outside chance I'm right."

"I'll take the bet if you will, too." Her sugary tone made him growl softly. "What about her?" She pointed to a pretty redhead in a low-cut dress, already regretting the impulse that made her try to turn the tables. "The two of you would contrast nicely. I'm sure you could come to an understanding that would last thirty days."

His features resembled stone as he did the first shot. He nudged the second shot glass toward her then pointed to the guy in the sweater vest. "Tell me why you can't even consider, hypothetically, marrying that guy."

Lost for words, feeling strangely pressured, she grabbed a shot and forced it down.

"Him?" Ethan pointed at a sandy haired guy in jeans and a checked shirt. He had a ready smile, but the sheer number of empty beer glasses in front of him was a worry. She looked down at the shiny rows of tequila and grimaced. *Pot meet kettle.*

She picked up another shot, tilted it to catch the light, and then drank it in one swallow. "I might as well drink all of these now."

"All I'm asking is that you admit there's a possibility you'd be happy."

"With any man here?"

He nodded.

"And it's a bet, right?"

Another nod.

"If I lose, I wake up in my own private tequila hell. What do I get if I win?"

He frowned, rubbing his temple as if his head was as fuzzy and achy as hers. "You get the satisfaction of knowing you were right all along. Your plan was sound, you just chose the wrong co-pilot."

Whoa. It almost sounds as if you want the job. Her imagination went berserk as she thrust Ethan into the role he wanted filled. He'd said she could choose anyone here, so why not him? The look of horror on his face ought to make her suggestion worthwhile.

She turned her barstool toward him and carefully slid off it, resting her hands on the smooth wool of his suit pants as she stepped between his knees. The position mirrored what he'd done earlier, except this time she had control. The temptation to slide her hands higher and press closer proved impossible to resist. She did a little of each, swaying despite the flat slippers on her feet. Her head pounded, clouding her vision. She smiled up at Ethan, captivated anew by his strong jawline and the dimple in his chin.

"You're probably right. If I knew the deal would expire in thirty days, I could be happy with anyone. Even you." She savored his absolute bewilderment, thrilled that she'd thrown him for a loop. "I believe this is yours?"

He swallowed heavily, regarding the shot glass in her hand as if it might morph into a mystical creature at any moment. Without a word he took it and drank it. When he reached for the next one, she stopped him.

"You don't have to drink any more. And don't look so panicked at the reprieve. I won't hold you to anything. I know the last thing you want is a wife."

"It couldn't hurt," he said in a low voice. "A pretty wife by my side in court during my parents' divorce wouldn't be the worst thing."

Just how drunk was he? His speech wasn't slurred, but his eyelids were heavy and his touch was uncharacteristically bold. She knew how that felt. Her hands seemed to be sliding over him with a familiarity they shouldn't possess. If she were sober she'd exercise more restraint. Tequila gave her courage to enjoy the man and the moment. He felt so good beneath her hands, against her breasts, mmm, digging into her stomach. She squirmed, unable to get close enough. Kissing helped. She slid her arms around him, rising up on her tiptoes and sliding her body over his.

He pulled the ponytail holder out and looped her hair around one wrist, controlling the angle of her head while he deepened their kiss. The other people in the bar seemed to fade away, but when a glass smashed nearby, Ethan pulled away. His look of apology told her the fun was over. Damn, it was a shame they weren't closer to their hotel. She'd just begun to appreciate Ethan as a man and a potential lover, and now he was retreating behind his tour guide persona. She sighed. In a few hours these delicious moments would be nothing more than a dim memory.

• • •

Ethan awoke with a splitting headache and a vague memory of Sara coming on to him after doing a bunch of tequila shots. *Sara.* He tried to sit up, whimpering like a wounded animal as gravity and light assaulted his senses. With his eyes closed he took stock of his situation. He was in bed, naked, and couldn't remember getting there. He lifted his hand and swiped his palm over his face, scraping it with the edge of something. What the *hell* was that on his finger?

He cracked one eye open and regarded the simple gold band in horror.

Surely not?

He flipped onto his side, ignoring the rising nausea and the debilitating stab of pain through his head. They wouldn't kill him, but Sara might.

She stirred as if on cue, probably suffering from motion sickness after he'd bounced the mattress. Dear God, let her be fully dressed and playing a prank by putting a cheap band on his finger and sliding into bed beside him.

Her eyelids fluttered, blinking slowly as she transitioned from slumber to wakefulness. "Ethan?"

The alarm in her tone was genuine. She scrunched the covers up to her neck, a gold band winking at him from her left hand. *Damn.*

"I don't understand."

"Me either." He kept his tone gentle and forced himself to think rationally. Hell if he knew how they'd ended up here together, apparently married, but Sara needed him to be the voice of calm and reason. He could sense how close to the surface her emotions were. He wasn't in any condition to deal with them. "Let's take care of our hangovers first, okay?"

Pain contorted her features when she tried to lift her head off the pillow.

"Okay."

His conscience twisted, her quiet misery biting deep. Gritting his teeth, he sat up, careful to keep the covers in place. Rehydration was a must, so his first call was to a company he'd used before. They specialized in administering hydrating infusions via IV, and he was relatively sure they provided in-room treatments.

When he hung up after arranging for immediate service, Sara groaned softly.

"Now I'm really confused," she said. "I didn't know that instant hangover cures existed. They must be one of those 'only in Vegas' things."

He smiled, proud of the way she was holding it together.

"They're available elsewhere too, but I think there's a bigger call for them here. How are you feeling? You're welcome to use the bathroom." He stared at her when she didn't respond. "Sara?"

"You're stalling," she said quietly. "We need to talk."

"We need our damn heads screwed on straight before we talk."

She recoiled from his harsh tone, her eyes squinting as if the pain of moving was too much to bear. Protective instincts that only seemed to be triggered by her rushed to the fore, crippling him with helplessness. He couldn't help her until the IV attendants arrived.

"Try not to worry," he said. "We'll work this out."

A low moan of distress slipped through her lips, and she pushed her head deeper into the pillows. She dragged her knees up to her chest and hugged them, struggling to comfort herself.

That's my job. You're my wife.

He pushed his territorial thoughts aside and made another phone call to arrange for over the counter painkillers to be delivered to their suite. Easing Sara's physical discomfort had to be his first play here. He tried to imagine what else she might want, his discarded suit pants supplying an obvious answer. He stepped into them, doing his best not to sway as he looked down at her.

"I'll get you some water then I'll help you to the bathroom if you need me to. One step at a time, okay?"

She didn't speak until he'd turned away. "Ethan?" Her voice dropped to a near-whisper. "I'm naked under here."

He willed his voice to hide most of what was going on inside his head. "No worries. There's a robe in the bathroom." He left before she could say another word.

When he returned she was sitting up in bed with the covers clutched to her chest and her head tipped back against the padded bedhead. She didn't move a muscle, not even when he sat on the edge of the bed.

"Water?"

The confusion in her eyes made him feel lower than he had in a very long time.

She gestured between them. "Is this real? Do you remember—anything?"

"Shots." He shrugged. "Making out in the bar. Maybe a taxi. Then I woke up here."

Unsteady hands reached for the glass and she gulped some water.

"I'm married," she said. "To you." A range of diverse emotions flitted across her face, underscored by the nausea she couldn't hide. "What time is it?"

"Two fifteen."

"Oh." For almost a minute she mulled that over. "I wasn't supposed to get married until five."

The curses exploding through his head were scathing. This was meant to be Sara's wedding day, the culmination of almost twenty years of planning, and an ultimate celebration of love and commitment. Instead, it was a farce. He should say something, but what good were words when your actions were unforgivable?

Color flared on her pale cheeks and she pressed the cool water against them before taking a shaky breath. "I need to ask you something."

"Anything."

"Last night…" She laughed anxiously. "Did you use protection?"

The bottom fell out of his world. Blood pounded through his veins, and time suspended as the pressure in his head built.

Sara's slender fingers curled around his bicep and squeezed, bringing his attention back to her. "It's important, Ethan. Remember that big, fancy, pointless party I planned with my ex?" She waited for him to nod. "He and I wanted to start a family straightaway, on our honeymoon, so I'm not on the pill."

Chapter Nine

Ethan's stunned silence told Sara everything she needed to know: he hadn't been careful, and the *only* thing he wanted from her was a quick and painless divorce.

"Not your problem," she said stiffly. "Don't worry about it. You need to move so I can get up and shower."

In a flash he'd leaned across her and planted his hand beside her hip, trapping her in place.

"If there's a chance you're pregnant, it's definitely my — concern. At the moment I'm concentrating on basic necessities like breathing. What do you say we give each other a bit of leeway while we claw our way back to humanity?" His jaw tightened when she tried to interrupt. "We made some decisions last night that impact both of our lives. We're going to have to pull together. Agreed?"

A slight tilt of her head was all she could manage. Ethan's lawyer mode was more than she could handle right now.

"Bathroom." Her voice was a mere squeak as she battled

a fresh wave of nausea. "*Please.*"

He picked her up, covers and all, and deposited her in the bathroom with most of her modesty intact. She cuddled his supportive arm, reluctant to let go, so damn grateful for his presence that her knees began to shake. No one had ever taken care of her when she was sick. She glanced up at Ethan, surprised by his level of concern for her when he was suffering from the same affliction. His skin had a grey tinge to it and his eyes were more bloodshot than blue.

"How do you feel? You look awful. What I mean is…"

"It's safe to say I feel the way I look." He steadied her and backed away. "Shut the door, but don't lock it, okay? Call if you need me."

The spacious room felt empty without him. She wavered uncertainly before sliding the door closed and releasing her hold on the covers draped around her. Carefully avoiding her reflection, she splashed some cold water on her face and debated the wisdom of stepping away from the basin.

Get it together, Greaves. Hurry up.

Her gaze swung to the mirror, staring at the ghostly pale woman with tense features, wild hair, and no clothes. Man, she was in serious need of some TLC.

Twenty minutes later she stared at the bathroom door wishing she had the guts to go through it. In a hotel robe, her hair twisted into a messy topknot, she looked okay, but how was she supposed to face Ethan after her earlier rudeness?

A knock at their door gave her the courage to scoot out of the bathroom and past Ethan who was on his way to answer it. His hand slipped into hers, halting her progress. Feeling incredibly unsure of herself, she sent him a questioning look.

"Wow." He squeezed her fingers with slight pressure.

"You're a knockout."

Her pleasure faded when she realized he was feeding her a line. She'd elevated her look to 'vaguely human' but he'd chosen a pretty lie over a genuine compliment.

"Thank you." She bit the words out. "You should get the door."

"Sara?" He hesitated, cursing softly when the knock sounded again. "The morning after is a new experience for me because I don't do sleepovers. Ever. I don't share—"

"Intimacies?" She wished the word back as soon as she'd said it. Sex was intimate and he clearly didn't have a problem with that.

He stepped toward her, until his face almost touched hers. "I don't usually share a bathroom, a robe, my bed, or any kind of conversation before breakfast. You're the exception to every rule. You might want to cut me some slack."

The next few hours were a blur of pleasantries and calming experiences. Ethan spent a good deal of his time talking quietly into his cell phone, making call after call, sneaking worried glances at her that seemed to intensify as the day wore on. She didn't know who he was talking to, but she was content to let everything drift past her, accepting tepid water, headache tablets, and fresh clothing from her room without question.

When Ethan told her she had to laze on the couch and watch sitcoms while the hydrating IV worked its magic, she simply nodded. Organizing everyone to within an inch of their lives was usually her role, but today it was easier to follow Ethan's lead.

She blinked at him after the nurse left, surprised to see him looking tense.

"Oh, didn't it work for you?"

"It worked."

His tone wasn't welcoming. She flicked her tongue across her lips and tried again.

"Well, *I* feel amazing right now, except I'm crazy hungry. I'm going to order one of everything from room service. Wanna share?"

A wide smile transformed his face.

"Welcome back. You had me worried there for a while." He chuckled softly. "If you don't know why, don't stress about it." He checked his watch and gave her a probing look. "I've got dinner covered. What you want isn't available from room service, so I've arranged for a local restaurant to prepare it and deliver it at six."

She shuddered involuntarily. Something was a little off about his dinner plans, but she couldn't decide what. Before she could question him, their order arrived. And it was big!

Two uniformed men each set a multitude of items on the dining table, then stepped back to discreetly wait for a tip. She jumped up to take care of it, tossing her handbag on the floor near the door after they'd gone.

Ethan padded over to her, barefoot, and slid to his knees. He held both of her hands, apparently unaware that her heart was tripping wildly and she was having trouble breathing.

"We seem to have skipped every milestone prior to this, and believe me when I say I'm more surprised than you to find myself married. Getting an annulment isn't our only choice."

"Yeah, it is."

"You could *choose* to spend a month in LA with me. I live in Malibu, right on the beach." He held his hands up. "It's an obligation-free offer. Separate everything except kitchen. Our marriage doesn't have to be a mistake. We can decide how it will play out."

She shook her head.

"Commitment isn't my thing. I've already spent longer with you than any other woman, yet I'm not ready to walk away. I know you're free. Would it be so bad to spend a month with me?"

"Last night—"

"Doesn't have to set the tone. Will I try to seduce you? Hell yeah, but you'll like what I have in mind." A strangely vulnerable expression crossed his face. "Let me show you what I mean. I want our first meal together as husband and wife to be perfect."

That same feeling of trepidation assailed her again. Their marriage, while apparently legal, wasn't real. So why was he acting like their future depended on him getting every detail right?

"There's a dress on a hanger in the bathroom. Why don't you slip that on while I dish up?" Her stunned silence seemed to amuse him. He raised her left hand to his mouth and placed a kiss over her wedding ring. "Go."

She took a long look at the space where his knees met the carpet, rocked by a feeling of injustice. Men usually knelt before women this way when they had a profound declaration to share. Ethan didn't feel that way about her. *Nobody* did. Gabe had done the things she'd expected of him, much as she'd done for Ethan today. She could see now that Gabe had been drawn to the picture-perfect life she'd planned. That's what he'd wanted, not her.

A sick sense of dread whispered that maybe Ethan wanted that life, too. Sentimentality and tradition weren't things she associated with him, but here in this moment he was embracing both. Panic ran through her veins as her past and future collided head on. She couldn't handle Ethan slipping seamlessly into Gabe's place. What if she'd made this happen? Last night was a giant blur, but it had been her last chance to bag a fiancé and remain on schedule. Had she grabbed that chance?

"Sara?" The sharpness of Ethan's tone suggested it wasn't the first time he'd said her name. "It's time to dress for dinner."

She tugged her hands free and escaped to the bathroom for a few blissful moments of seclusion. What greeted her was almost enough to make her turn around and leave. Crap. What were the odds of Ethan choosing a dress so freakin' similar to her "going away" dress? Trying not to read too much into the coincidence, she quickly changed, and added a dash of lipstick and the dangly earrings Ethan had left on the counter. On a whim she redid her hair, neatening the topknot and securing it with dozens of bobby pins.

"It's just dinner," she told her reflection. "Stop looking for hidden meanings."

When she walked into the dining room, Ethan's eyes heated the same way they had that first night in the beauty salon.

"You look beautiful."

She shrugged awkwardly. "Even though you had all my

stuff sent up, I don't have any shoes that match."

He grinned and waved a bare foot toward her. "You match me." He pointed at the table. "Grab a seat. You'd already decided on a menu for tonight, so I've tried to replicate it."

Her gaze skated over a platter containing individual salmon and leek tartlets, miniature crab cakes, stuffed mushrooms, and drizzled figs draped in prosciutto. She gripped a chair back, knuckles whitening as she tried to make sense of what she was seeing. The dishes were all firm favorites. She'd planned to serve them at her wedding reception. How the hell did Ethan know that? And why was he torturing her with a connection that shouldn't exist? A rush of tears blinded her as she was forced to acknowledge all of the things that today should have held, but hadn't.

"Ethan, I—" She waved her hands, unsure what she'd say if her vocal chords were in working order, knowing only that she hurt in places that might never recover.

"I know your wedding day was supposed to be flawless from start to finish. I can't give you that, but I made a few calls to ensure the food, at least, is perfect." Ethan smiled and pulled her chair out for her. "Don't worry about the cost of pulling this together at short notice. You're welcome."

She was *welcome*? When her brain finally decided on a course of action it was swift and decisive. She bolted for the door of the suite, grabbing her handbag along the way. In the hall she dashed for the elevator, slipping into it just as the doors slid closed.

• • •

Ethan didn't make the elevator in time. Shit. He'd locked himself out of the room. He had no money or identification or *shoes*. And his barefoot bride was running amok on the Vegas Strip without him.

Anger, fear, and confusion slammed into him like combination punches from a world-class fighter. He'd *promised* her she'd be happy if she married any guy in the bar last night, and then he'd stepped up and nabbed the job for himself. Despite his good intentions, he'd gotten it so wrong on day one that she'd run away from him. Sara, who could hold her own in an argument against him better than any non-lawyer he'd ever met, had fled without a word.

Damn it all to hell, if she was upset enough to drive home to Utah, she'd discover what he'd found out earlier in the day when he'd called all the wedding venues in Sara's hometown asking about her intended menu for the reception. Surprising her with the exact menu she'd chosen had seemed like the perfect way to ensure that her carefully laid plans weren't all for naught. If this one thing turned out right, then she wouldn't feel as if she'd missed the whole event. It was meant to be a positive for her to hold on to, instead he'd learned that her wedding had gone ahead as planned. Her bastard of an ex had hijacked it, substituting the bride for one more to his liking at the last minute. What a poor excuse for a human being that guy must be.

He slammed his fist against the elevator button before roaring out his frustration, startling a couple further down the hall as they exited their suite. Crap. Maybe he'd be wise to take one flight of stairs down then catch the elevator from there? Hell, he didn't even know where Sara would go. The big ball they'd been invited to was on tonight at the Masquerade Hotel. When he'd first mentioned it, Sara had seemed fascinated by the idea of attending, but with no shoes, no partner, and no tickets, he was confident she'd give it a miss. She was hungry, though, so hopefully eating would be at the top of her to-do list.

He reached the stairwell and began to race downstairs, glad to be doing something constructive. Sara would probably look for a casual restaurant with a high turnover of customers, the kind of place where her bare feet and lack of company might go unnoticed. Eight floors later he burst out of the stairwell and headed for the elevator. Running was cathartic, but he couldn't spare the time for another twenty flights of stairs.

He checked the most obvious places first, anywhere that might be familiar to her. When there was no sign of her, he checked at the reservations desk to see if she'd requested access to their suite or booked another one. She hadn't. Drinking was out, he couldn't imagine her gambling alone, and in her current state of mind she'd want to avoid interacting with people as much as possible.

He ignored the curious stares that his custom tailored suit and bare feet were garnering. Only one person in Vegas mattered. Finding her ranked above breathing. Would she leave Vegas without saying goodbye, without her suitcase or her car?

Her car.

Sara had chosen the hotel's self-park option, which only made her car that much more appealing an escape route. She knew exactly where it was. She wouldn't have to wait for someone to bring it to her, or have a plan for where to go once she had it. She could simply climb into a comfortable, familiar space and lock the world out. As he catalogued all the positives he started to run.

He was glad now that she'd shown him a photo of her car on her phone. When he finally located the blue Golf with Utah plates, Sara wasn't in it. Unwilling to walk away without taking action, he scanned the surrounding area then let the air out of all four tires. Vandalism and a law degree didn't make good bedfellows, but she was worth the risk.

Chapter Ten

Sara's entire life plan had dwindled to one thing: a search for seclusion. She didn't care if she had to sit in a toilet cubicle all night to get it. The look on Ethan's face had promised retribution as the elevator door closed between them, but even that was a worry for another time.

While the elevator made its descent she dug through her bag for her cell phone. Finding her spa slippers stuffed in the side pocket she paused to put them on, and then resumed her search.

The one person who *might* understand how gutted she felt tonight was Gabe. They weren't in love, she appreciated that distinction now, but this was the day that would have changed both their lives forever. Touching base with him would help to ground her. If he hadn't dumped her, she wouldn't be in Vegas, so ruining his night was her prerogative. She called his number as she left the elevator, silently willing him to pick up.

He wasn't home. Disappointed, she headed for the street exit. The line for taxis was too long, so she started walking, searching for a restaurant that wouldn't balk at her slippers. She found one, sat in a quiet corner, and ordered soup and crusty bread. While waiting for it to arrive she called Gabe's cell, followed by everyone in her address book. No one answered. Not one person. She tried not to think it, she really did, but what if the entire town had gathered to celebrate Gabe's near miss?

She scowled into her soup bowl, mentally reviewing things Ethan had let slip over the past few days. He was the only child of feuding parents. By his own admission he'd never had a real relationship, and he'd come to Vegas alone. Crap, why did it suddenly feel as if she was the center of his world? She called the hotel, intending to leave a message for Ethan, then had a change of heart at the last second.

"Hi, if possible I'd like to book a room with two beds for immediate check-in. I'm almost at the hotel now. The deluxe queen has two queen size beds? That would be fabulous, thank you." She gave her name and cringed when it was a match for both Ethan's suite and the room she'd given up earlier. "It's complicated. If you could just organize this one last room for me, I promise I won't bother you again." When the booking was confirmed she asked to be connected to Ethan's suite. She wasn't shocked to discover he was out.

She dragged her feet on the way back to the hotel, debating what to tell Ethan. A lot would depend on his attitude, but she wanted him to know she was safe. In the end she asked the reservation clerk to put a notation beside his name. If he contacted the desk for any reason they'd advise him of her new accommodations. In the meantime, she'd call his suite from her room and leave a careful apology for running out on him. She didn't know him well enough to anticipate his state of mind, but she was willing to concede a few points to get negotiations underway.

· · ·

Ethan replayed Sara's message over and over. Returning to their suite alone, after his recent criminal actions, he'd hoped to grab a quick bite to eat. He'd planned to follow that up with an extended search of Vegas—while wearing shoes.

Adjusting his mindset to this new reality was going to take one hell of an effort. He needed to be damn sure of himself before he contacted Sara. If he wasn't careful, she'd read too much into his concern for her and start thinking he cared.

He wanted Sara as his wife for the thirty days they'd discussed. Imagining her naked was a constant problem because his memory of last night was hazy, but sex was only part of the equation. He'd jam his hands in his pockets for the entire month if she'd let him do simple things like buy flowers and share meals. The benefits of having a pretty wife on his arm during his parents' divorce were numerous, but cheap stunts weren't his style. He'd prefer to keep their marriage between the two of them. His house was off limits to everyone, without exception, so no one would bother Sara if she stayed. It was also a rent-free option for her, and conveniently situated right on the beach. He could clear out his gym and conference room and give Sara the downstairs area to live and work in for a month.

Last night they'd made a drunken commitment. Now that they were sober, he could see its potential. Since meeting

Sara he'd begun to feel dissatisfied with the solitary monotony of his life. He liked spending time with her. She was at a loose end, her calendar free for the entire month because of her cancelled wedding. She couldn't go back to Utah. Her ex would either be there, or he'd be on her honeymoon with his new wife, and every one of her friends and neighbors would know. Living among them would be a nightmare before the truth surfaced. Afterward, she'd have to leave.

Despite LA's drawbacks—his job, his parents, and his shallow friends—Sara would be better off relocating to LA for the thirty-day marriage they'd agreed upon. He'd have someone in his life for the first time ever, and she'd have a chance to mourn the death of her dreams without encountering her ex or his new wife. Hell, if he ensured her business flourished in LA, she might relocate permanently.

He rubbed his palms over his face, already contemplating who to call to set that in motion. LA thrived on blatantly sexy lingerie—black, skimpy, and daring. Was that the kind Sara designed? An image of the pale pink scraps of perfection he'd spied on the floor this morning flashed through his mind. Dear God, if LA women embraced Sara's ultra-feminine designs, she could buy a mansion in Malibu with change to spare.

And forget all about Utah.

Aware that he was getting ahead of himself, he dialed Sara's number. "I'll be at your door in five minutes. And Sara? You might want to order a limited supply of tequila shots, because I bet you're going to love LA." He disconnected before she could reply.

Twenty minutes later he watched her smooth forehead settle into deep creases.

"I don't understand."

"That's what you said first thing this morning."

She snorted. "I understand we let alcohol cloud our judgment last night and made a silly mistake. What I'm having trouble with, specifically, is your desire to compound that mistake by moving in together. You're as sober as I am." She leaned close as if to confirm that he didn't have alcohol on his breath. "What's really going on, Ethan?"

He'd planned this conversation carefully on his way down to her room. "Marriage and I weren't ever meant to be, yet here we are, married in Vegas. Walking away would be too easy. I prefer a challenge." He raised one finger off the counter, subtly requesting silence while he finished. "Last night I dared you to marry someone from the bar."

"I did!"

"I also said you'd be blissfully happy after thirty days." He grinned as realization dawned on her face.

"And you want to be right?" She dragged her lower lip into her mouth and worried it with her teeth, making a startled squeak when he freed it. "Is this really worth all the effort to you? Marriage to me might not be what you expect. It won't be like thirty dates strung together. Dressing up and going out is just a small part of it. It's also looking out for each other and being prepared to drop everything when you're needed. It's home cooked meals, curling up together on the sofa after a long day, sharing a b—"

"Bathroom?"

"I was going to say bed."

My wife is fearless. Most people would have taken the

easy out.

"If we stay together for thirty days, sex won't be part of the equation."

"But you'll cook for me?" he said teasingly. "In my home, late at night, wearing my ring and something you've made earlier in the day."

She burst out laughing. "Anyone ever tell you—"

"Frequently."

She tilted her head to one side and studied him. "You're serious about this? Can I ask why?"

"I've never had a home life…" Embarrassment swamped him, but he sensed Sara waiting for him to open up more. He looked at her and said the only thing he could think of. "I want to. With you."

Instead of answering, she got up from her perch on the end of one of the beds and came to stand behind him. Her gentle fingers stayed on his shoulder when he began to turn toward her. A moment later her arms encircled him, hugging fiercely, her soft breasts pillowed against his back.

"Hm." She tipped her hands as if she was weighing choices. "Go back to Utah where it's freezing cold and deal with the aftermath of a wedding that never happened, or spend a month in sunny Malibu cooking late night snacks for you." She laughed. "There's no contest. The month's yours if you want it."

Turning rapidly, he pulled her down to sit on his lap, sealing their deal with a heated kiss that was just getting interesting when she eased away. He couldn't decide if thirty days were going to fly by, or if this would be the longest, horniest month of his life.

Chapter Eleven

Ethan promised a carefree month by the beach. He didn't deliver.

Over the next few days he tried to control every aspect of their so-called marriage.

"Butt out, would you?" She almost laughed at his look of horror. "You're being overbearing. Having my workspace in Utah packed up and shipped here was your idea. I know it's a lot to organize, but I can handle it. If you want to help, I'll delegate something to you."

He grinned. "We have an early dinner reservation in Newport Beach. It's about an hour away."

She shook her head, thrilled he'd booked it, yet annoyed at the same time. She'd have to drop what she was doing. Another romantic dinner was good though. If she didn't think too hard about it, she could almost believe that Ethan's caring husband charade was the real deal.

"Why do you keep working from home?" she asked as

they drove to the restaurant. "You go to the office, but you never stay more than a couple of hours. Don't they miss you?"

"Yeah."

The single, heavily spoken word surprised her. "Um, stop slacking off then, and get back to your usual schedule. I can entertain myself."

The words came easily, but as time passed by, the reality of long hours alone was harder to take. Ethan's work hours grew longer and longer. She didn't have any clients, any pending orders, any friends to catch up with, or more significantly, any wedding preparations to take care of.

She'd been wedding-obsessed most of her life, she saw that now, but her dreams had brought their whole community together. She missed that camaraderie. Being isolated in paradise with only Ethan for company was getting her down. The lights of the Santa Monica Pier were visible farther up the beach, but it, like her handsome husband, seemed unreachable. Since she'd given him permission to return to his regular hours, Ethan had practically lived at the office. When he was home he acted weirdly—pulling her chair out, topping up her wine glass, asking if she had everything she needed, if she was happy.

She had a spacious, light-filled place to work and a gorgeous guest room, but nothing to do all day. She'd assumed Ethan would introduce her to some potential clients. He hadn't. When he took her out to eat, it was always just the two of them on a private balcony or deserted beach, or else he chose a restaurant a long way from home where they'd be unlikely to encounter anyone he knew. Why had he brought her here if he didn't intend to introduce her to his friends and family? If he was ashamed of her, or embarrassed to admit he was married, she wished he'd say so.

She pushed away from her sewing machine and debated whether to change before heading down to the beach. As she went outdoors and walked toward the water's edge, she realized it didn't matter what she wore; she might as well be invisible for all the notice anyone took of her. The locals were so self-involved they didn't even acknowledge her when she spoke to them. She huffed out a sigh, staring at the red rubber ball that had rolled to a stop near her feet. Back in Utah she wouldn't hesitate to pick it up and toss it back, calling out a greeting as she did so. The exchange that followed wouldn't be scintillating, but it was better than the chill silence LA offered.

"Don't worry, honey, she's friendly."

The sugary sweet voice startled her, and moments later a giant black dog sprayed sand all over her as it pounced on the ball. She laughed as the dog bounded around in a circle then dropped the ball at her feet, before sitting up straight and barking expectantly.

"Well, aren't you gorgeous?" She bent to pick up the ball.

"I wouldn't do that."

Sara smiled at the Barbie doll clone who'd called out. "There's no such thing as throwing it once, huh?"

"Petra's spoiled rotten," the woman said as she jogged to a halt. "I'm watching her for the day and my arm's already aching from too many throws." She took the ball from Sara and tossed it without even looking. "I'm Zoe, by the way. I live about twelve doors down, in that slate-gray house."

"Sara." She pointed to Ethan's house right behind them.

"This is me. Temporarily."

Zoe's eyes widened, her gaze raking over Sara as if something didn't make sense. "You're with Ethan?"

Am I with him? Why does it sound as if you have more than just a passing interest?

"I'm, um, staying with him. He's letting me use a couple of rooms so I can work while I'm here."

Zoe wrestled the ball away from Petra and threw it into the shallows. "Are you prepping for a big case?" Zoe grinned at her silence. "What do you do, Sara?"

"I design lingerie."

"For real?" Zoe's interest level shot up. "Do you ever do one-off custom pieces?"

"It's mostly what I do."

"Right, let me just take Petra home. Wait, is Ethan's back garden secure? Petra could hang out there for a while." Zoe stopped suddenly and laughed. "You look a little scared. This is LA, honey. Good stuff tends to be fleeting, so we jump on it immediately. Speak up if that doesn't work for you." She threw the ball again. "So, Sara, are you free for the next hour?"

Sara grinned. "Sure. C'mon in. I'll show you some photos of previous commissions, plus what I'm working on now, and you can get a feel for what I do, see if it's for you."

Sara was stunned by Zoe's enthusiasm. They'd been at this for hours, discussing possibilities for different styles, fabrics, and trims.

"I can't believe you made all these things from scratch."

"I didn't. Well, I made some of them. I have a small team of employees back in Utah. They do most of the sewing."

Zoe looked taken aback. "Business is so good that you employ people. Wow. These negligees, particularly the baby doll ones, are fantastic. And you're saying I can have them made to my exact specifications? So if I wanted something to cling to my breasts and succumb to gravity if I *breathed* too deeply, you could make that happen?"

Sara fought the urge to smile. "Of course. What you're describing is a special occasion piece. You'll probably want something more practical for the following morning."

"Oh." Zoe's eyes lit up. "You're good at the soft sell. I feel as if you're genuinely trying to help me."

"I am!"

Zoe laughed, yet she was shaking her head at the same time. "LA's all about the hard sell. Everything's thrust in the consumer's face and there's an element of haste, a subtle threat that the deal will vanish unless it's accepted imme-diately. Your approach is the exact opposite, yet it's surpris-ingly effective. I can easily see myself ordering dozens of items." She stood and casually stripped her T-Shirt off. "You need measurements, right?"

Sara grabbed her tape measure and the conversation moved on to her dream of buying a 3D body scanner to take precise measurements. She was halfway through a sentence when Zoe suddenly gasped.

"What is *that*?"

That would be my wedding ring.

"It's just something new that I'm trying out."

Zoe stared at her with a look of wonder. "How new?"

"Eleven days."

"And you've been here…"

"Ten days. We came straight from Vegas."

Zoe's shriek hurt Sara's eardrums. "Holy crap, Sara. You've been holding out on me. And Ethan hasn't said a word to James."

"James?"

Zoe's exuberance vanished. "James Clayton? My brother. Ethan's best friend and partner in the law firm." She swore as Sara's shoulders rose and fell. "Whoa! How well do you know Ethan?"

Sara's mind reeled from the unexpected questions. "Not as well as I'd hoped. We've agreed to spend a month together, and we're working things out as we go. LA's a bit of an adjustment for me, but I'm okay, mostly."

Zoe studied her closely. "You're okay except for being confused and lonely, living with a man you barely know, and feeling out of place in a new city?" She snorted. "Listen, I don't know why Ethan's head's so far—"

Sara grinned. "Neither do I."

Zoe laughed. "If he hasn't told James about you, then it's time we fixed that. What do you say we all go out to dinner? I'll give James a call."

Sara shot her hand forward to rest on Zoe's cell phone.

"Let's eat here." She checked the time and grimaced. "You'd best warn James that it won't be fancy, unless he can steer his car toward a traffic jam to help me out?"

Zoe laughed and made the call. "Ethan's still at the office, but James just left," she said after she disconnected. "He's on his way, and as you heard, I didn't give him much of a heads-up. All he knows is that it's dinner for four, and not a night he'll want to miss. I'm going to run Petra home and feed her, dress for dinner, and grab a bottle of wine. I'll be back before James gets here." She hugged Sara close. "Don't worry. He's going to love you."

Sara didn't share Zoe's certainty, but if she wanted to have something to serve her guests then she'd better stop speculating and get cooking. She dragged a tub of vanilla ice cream out of the freezer to soften. Dessert would be easy, but her dinner options were limited. She turned the oven on, wondering what ingredients she had available that she could turn into a meal for four people within an hour.

Maybe Zoe would return in time to set the table, or fold the crushed candy bars through the ice cream and press it into the individual Jell-O molds she'd found in the bottom drawer. Almost everything in the kitchen was unused, still sealed in plastic. She tried not to wonder why.

A knock at the back door a little while later sent relief crashing through her. She raced over to it, and yanked the door open, calling out instructions over her shoulder as she headed back to the kitchen.

"I'm glad you're here. I could really use your help. How are you at mashing avocado?"

A masculine chuckle made her jump.

"I've never tried it, but I'm sure I'll manage."

She turned slowly, and then rapidly assessed the smiling, dark haired man who looked nothing at all like Zoe.

"James?" She gulped in some much needed air when he nodded. "I'm making a fabulous first impression," she muttered. "I'm Sara. I've spent most of the day with Zoe, and she thought you might want to know…" She shrugged and held up her left hand to show him her ring.

"She thought right." His voice held an ominous tone, but

he was looking at her like he was a kid at Christmas and she was the pony he'd asked for. "Your name's Sara?"

She nodded, bracing herself for any eventuality.

Gentle arms embraced her. "It's very nice to meet you, Sara."

• • •

Ethan followed his nose to the kitchen, fresh strawberries in one hand and a huge bunch of gerbera daisies in the other. He almost dropped the lot when he saw who was in the kitchen with Sara. What the hell were James and Zoe doing here? He didn't know what to say to them, so he focused on Sara.

"Berries for breakfast." He smiled at her and set them on the counter. "I thought you might want to make crepes since you missed out on the last lot."

"And those?" James pointed at the flowers. "What about them, *Romeo*?"

Sara's gaze shifted between the two of them.

"You wait until you're in the middle of the biggest case of your career and—"

Sara snatched the flowers out of Ethan's hands and thrust them at James.

"You can put those in a vase. There's one on the top shelf of the pantry. If you're not up for pleasant dinner conversation then I'll be happy to see you out. You can take your food to go."

No one spoke for the longest time, and then James smirked.

"I mashed the avocado for the guacamole, Zoe did that thing with the Jell-O molds, and you cooked. What has

Ethan done to contribute? Shouldn't he be the one to go?"

Ethan would have paid to avoid this confrontation. It was obvious that James thought his timing sucked, but if everyone had kept to themselves the way they were meant to, this quiet, temporary marriage could have worked. Now that their secret was out, his only thought was to protect Sara from James' sarcasm.

To his surprise, Sara spoke before he could.

"Vase. Pantry. Then amazing guacamole. Try to keep up, James."

She turned away, slipping her hands into heatproof gloves and withdrawing a pan of fragrant nachos from the oven. As she carried it into the dining room, James spoke to Ethan in a low voice.

"You bastard. I know your views on marriage, yet you've got the sweetest woman in the world wearing your ring and believing you're committed to her."

"She knows I'm not. It's temporary. We have a deal."

"She's a sweetheart, yet you just *happen* to be married to her while the media spotlight is on you. I know your parents' divorce is the biggest case of your career, but it won't be won outside the courtroom." James shoved the flowers against Ethan's chest. "I expected more from you. If this is who you've become, I'll be glad to represent Sara when you split."

Chapter Twelve

Sara watched the interplay between Ethan and James as the evening progressed. As best friends and business partners the two men should have been comfortable with each other. Instead, there were undercurrents she didn't understand, and they were worsening.

"Enough!" She set her dessert spoon down and turned her attention to James. "If you've got something to say, please just say it." She smiled encouragingly. "I'll try not to be offended that I'm not up to the standard of wife you imagined for Ethan."

Zoe got to her feet and glared at her brother until he stood too. "Sara," she said. "That's not what's going on."

"It's okay." Sara rubbed her tired eyes. "I'm not insulted. I'm aware that I don't belong here in LA, or with Ethan, so you're not telling me anything I don't know."

Ethan reached across the table to cover her hand with his.

"You *should* be offended. James is way out of line. He knows it, and he's leaving." Ethan switched his focus to Zoe. "Zoe, if you wouldn't mind?"

The brother and sister pair made their excuses and left quietly.

Ethan came to sit beside Sara and touched his fingertips to her lips. In the silence that followed he removed the bobby pins from her hair, one by one, and unwound her topknot. She sighed as he released her ponytail and began to massage her scalp with long, capable fingers.

"Zoe's right, Sara. James has a problem with me, not you."

She quivered beneath his hands, moaning appreciatively as his thumbs stroked her nape. "While you're doing that, I want to agree with whatever you say."

"Zoe loves your designs."

"Mmm, I know."

"James thinks you're an amazing cook."

"Mmm, he must be easily pleased."

"Sara?"

"Mmm?"

"I like having you here."

She sat up so fast her head spun.

"You're such a bad liar. When you suggested we shoot for a whole month of wedded bliss, I thought you were crazy, but it felt like something you needed to do. It's not though, is it? You're obviously not willing to introduce me to your family and friends, so why did you bring me here? It's confusing. On the one hand you're adding candles to the dinner table, constantly fussing with my wine glass, and buying flowers and berries, and on the other you're hoping no one ever learns of our connection."

"Sara—"

"When you arrived home tonight and discovered we had company, you looked almost scared."

"James is my best friend. He…" For a moment she thought he'd finished. "We work together. There are client lunches, and the occasional gala. Sometimes we surf."

"Work, lunch, surfing, got it." She sucked in a shallow breath when a wild thought occurred to her. "Are you trying to tell me that James hasn't been here before?"

He looked uncomfortable. "To drop files off."

If Ethan's home was off limits to his best friend, then her presence here held a whole wealth of importance. Ethan hadn't wanted to accept no for an answer once he'd extended the invitation for her to come and stay. She didn't know what that meant, exactly, but she sure as hell owed him an apology for tonight's impromptu dinner party. "Tonight was my fault. I thought…well, I guess I didn't think. Not enough, anyway. I'm sorry I didn't warn you."

Ethan stroked his knuckles down her cheek. "Don't be. Given the option, I'll always choose not to share. When I find something I like, my career, this house…"

Me?

"I build the highest wall I can around it and set up an exclusion zone."

"Sounds lonely."

Ethan pressed his lips against her temple. "It can be. Thank you for tonight. I've never had a dinner party before."

He'd barely touched his food and their guests left early. Surely that called for an upgrade? "I noticed you didn't eat much." She toyed with the top button on her shirt, half expecting him to lunge forward. "I can fix you something else."

He got to his feet and stared down at her with a peculiar mix of weariness and lust. "That's not a good idea. I don't think any of this is a good idea. I don't want to build a wall around you and isolate you from the rest of the world. If you stay much longer, I might."

She watched him walk away, praying she wasn't falling for her husband.

. . .

James was waiting in Ethan's office when he arrived the next morning. "Sara designs lingerie?"

"You're shouting. You want to take it down a notch?"

James' fists clenched. "What did you do, contact a dating service and confide every preference you've ever had: gorgeous, gullible, and guaranteed to be wearing hot, little panties? For chrissakes, Ethan, we're in the wrong profession to even *look* at someone like Sara. And she's not the kind of woman we'd ever get as a client. Do you know why? Because if a guy's lucky enough to marry her—"

"Last night was out of my hands. You weren't supposed to meet her. Ever."

James flicked his hand in an impatient gesture.

"It's complicated, and temporary, and if you wouldn't have done the same in my shoes, then you're no friend of mine."

"Tell me."

Ethan shook his head. "Let's just call my involvement… damage control. What do you know about insurance policies on events? Say, a dream wedding? If it's called off, they pay out because that's the deal, right? What do you think happens if the event goes ahead without the policyholder's participation?"

James threw himself into the closest chair. "Try again. Short sentences."

"Sara planned the wedding to end all weddings. Every expense covered by her, every detail perfect, everything that is, except for the groom. He dumped her two weeks before the big day, and although he promised to cancel everything immediately, he didn't follow through. Sara doesn't know that. She waited a week before filing a claim, and has been waiting for them to send her a check ever since. I called and told them I'm acting on her behalf. I gave them my contact number in lieu of hers so that they won't ambush her with news she's not expecting."

"What news?"

Ethan met James' eyes. "The wedding went ahead, on schedule with a different bride." He swiped his open palms over his face. "I've tried to assure her we'll handle it here at the office because it's the kind of thing we regularly do, but eventually she's going to contact the insurance company."

James closed his eyes and tapped one finger against his nose. "Where's the ex? Do you know?"

"Utah."

"Within driving distance of an airport?"

Ethan grinned. "Yeah."

He tilted his head toward the door and James nodded.

"Confirm he's there then book our flights. Call Sara and let her know you'll be working late."

Ethan nodded, but within a few minutes their trip to

Utah was off. Sara's ex was in Thailand on the perfect honeymoon Sara had planned. Crap. On impulse he picked up the phone and called Sara. It had been too long since he'd seen her, almost an hour.

"Hey, are you free for lunch?"

She laughed softly. "You can't be hungry. You just had two servings of crepes. Oh." He heard the change in her voice. "Have you and James had words already?"

"It's just lunch, Sara. Come into the city and eat with me."

"Midday?"

"Sure." He hung up, anticipation pumping through him. Unless he had a meeting with clients, he usually ate at his desk. Today was an exception. He was taking off work for a lunch date with his beautiful wife. *How odd is that*? he thought.

• • •

Zoe called Sara a couple of days later. "Can I stop by and confirm my order? I know we talked about the kinds of things I wanted, but I'm not certain I've actually placed an order. How's midday for you?"

All alone in her sunlit sewing room, Sara blushed.

"Ah, that's not so good. I've started to meet Ethan each day for a quick bite before his afternoon really takes off. I don't want to miss it, and I'm sure he's expecting me too."

Zoe's silence quickly became awkward.

"Okay, how about now? I have a friend, another neighbor, who turned positively green when I told her about your custom-made baby dolls. If we pop over in a few minutes can she have a look at some of your samples? Fair warning though, she's got deep pockets and she's going to want at least one of everything you show her."

"Sure. I'll see you soon."

The morning flew by in a blur of appreciative murmurs punctuated by the occasional squeal. Zoe brought two friends with her and they seemed to both want the same thing—delicate baby doll nightgowns in pastel shades. She wouldn't have thought much of it, except that their preferences mirrored Zoe's. They'd always been popular, in bridal white for weddings, but that clearly wasn't the case here.

She grabbed several samples on her way out the door, poking them into the tiny gift bag Ethan had arrived home with last night. The perfume it had contained then fit a lot better than the negligees, but she was already running late. She handed her car off to the valet at the hotel near Ethan's office and bolted inside his building. She caught her breath in the elevator, waved hello to his PA, who was on the phone, and burst into his office, full of apology for being a few minutes late. He looked startled…almost guilty.

"Ethan?" The woman's voice came from behind Sara, out of sight.

Sara froze at the disapproving tone. Why hadn't she considered that Ethan's closed door might mean he was with a client?

"I'm so sorry. Please excuse me."

"You're here now," the woman said. "And apparently you're late. Perhaps my son would care to explain why he has two appointments scheduled at once?"

Your son?

Sara sensed the floor rising up to meet her as the world

tilted dangerously. This woman had all the warmth of a Popsicle, and she was Ethan's mother?

Sara couldn't decipher the look Ethan sent her, but she had a bad feeling about it.

"Mother, this is Sara."

"Greaves." She winced at the abruptness of her tone, aware that she'd drawn attention to the very thing she was trying to smooth over.

Her feet refused to co-operate. Turning around was a must, so she persevered. She balanced her bag on the edge of Ethan's desk and extended her hand to the sour woman. Her greeting died in her throat when she realized Ethan's mother had no intention of shaking her hand. Just then there was a soft *plop*, and the look on the older woman's face confirmed her worst fears.

The bag had tipped and lingerie spilled out onto the floor. She'd wanted to know Ethan's thoughts on the sweetly sexy negligees, and she was about to find out.

Chapter Thirteen

Ethan's mother seemed to look everywhere at once, taking in Sara, the lingerie, and her son. "I see you have plans."

"Mrs. Munroe?" Sara felt the tension in the room ramp up and wished she had another way to address the woman. "This" —she pointed to the lingerie— "isn't anything to be concerned about. If I'd wanted to seduce Ethan on his lunch break, I'd have picked my favorite piece and worn it." She ignored Ethan's choking fit. "As it is, I've interrupted your meeting with Ethan. I'll go, and see him later for dinner."

Ethan's mother seemed to stare right through her. "The charity gala is tonight. You are going?"

Sara wasn't sure how to respond. It was the first she'd heard of it.

"Of course." Ethan flashed Sara another inscrutable look. "James has our tickets. Sara's just popped in to get them."

"And get a second opinion on which slip to wear beneath

her gown?"

Gown? Where the heck was she going to get one of those?

Ethan scooped the bag and its contents off the floor and smirked as one item unfurled. "If Sara's wearing something like this, we won't be staying long."

Sara snatched them out of Ethan's hand and called out a hasty farewell as she left. She couldn't believe Ethan was having that conversation with his mother, or that he'd signed them up for attendance at a fundraiser. For a man who supposedly wanted to keep their marriage quiet, he sure seemed to fail a lot.

She darted down the hall to James' office and poked her head through the open door. "I need help. Ethan's mother wants us to attend a function tonight."

"She wants you there?"

Sara stared at him. "I don't know what to do. Ethan says you have tickets. I'm going to need a heads-up on what to wear."

James studied her. "You've got more than clothing options on your mind. Is it Ethan?"

She exhaled as a wave of disillusionment swamped her. "I think he's losing sight of his objectives. I thought I was coming here to get a brief taste of his life, but he told me the other night, after you and Zoe left, that he never planned for anyone to know we were married. It was supposed to be our secret, one quiet month of play-acting followed by a discreet divorce. That made me feel like a dirty little secret to be kept hidden at all costs, but his new policy of introducing me to everyone as if I matter is even worse."

James didn't say anything. He didn't have to.

"I don't know how to play the games Ethan plays. He's

so busy trying to be the perfect partner that he forgets to be himself. Living with him is like being on a date that never ends. I keep waiting for him to relax enough to show me who he really is. I love the glimpses I'm getting, but they're usually fleeting, and I want so much more." She groaned, aware that she'd said too much already, yet unable to stop. "When he pretends to care, he's very convincing. Sometimes I wonder if—"

James' phone cut her off. *Good timing.*

She wrote *Zoe* on a blank sheet of paper, slid it across the desk toward him, and made her escape while he was busy.

• • •

Sara's elegant, deep red cocktail dress was no different than many of the others in the function room of the hotel, yet Ethan couldn't stop staring. His entire world was wrapped up in the woman in *this* dress. Every thought he had related to her in some way, and his career had become something unfortunate that dragged him away from her five days a week. He gathered her closer, tormenting himself with the constant brush of her body against his as they slow danced among LA's elite.

"We should do this every day."

Sara smiled up at him. "If we did, we'd lose what little sleep time we have."

"Sleeping's overrated."

In the space of a heartbeat the mood between them shifted, heating, promising untold delights if they gave it free rein. Ethan shifted closer. "Slip your arms around my neck."

He dropped his hands to her hips and held her still while he pressed against her, wincing slightly when her fingers tightened in his hair. "Tell me why we should stay here."

"Do you think anyone would notice if we left?"

"No."

He tugged her hand, directing her to the right as they slipped out a side entrance and stepped into a long hall.

She pulled him into the shadows midway between wall sconces, and rose up on her tiptoes, her soft body sliding against his.

"What if we didn't have to drive home tonight?"

The room card she pressed into his hand shattered the last of his resolve. Sara had expanded the boundaries of their marriage in the sweetest possible way. Everything she did was smooth and perfect, just like —

He halted the progress of his hand as it slid up her thigh, raising the modest hem of her dress to an indecent level. Hell, they had a room nearby. Surely he could wait till they got there to start undressing her?

"Where?"

She pointed and he dragged himself away from her long enough to stride down the hall, her small hand held tightly within his.

He flung the door to their room open and drew her inside, telling her what he needed before the door had fully closed.

"Dress. Off. Now."

Her throat shifted delicately as she swallowed. Without a word she reached for his hands and guided them to the side zipper of her dress.

She hadn't spoken, yet his mind supplied the phrase, *you*

do it.

He took a beat, the importance of this moment sinking in. If he wanted more than thirty days with Sara, he had to get this right. He lowered the zipper and lifted her dress up and over her head in one quick motion, aware that her lingerie would need to be appreciated at length. His control was usually rock solid, but it shook whenever he got close to Sara.

She stepped closer when he stared for too long without touching.

"Nice?"

Perfect breasts, encased in deep red satin, nudged against the black of his suit jacket. He smiled slowly and shook his head.

"Not nice. Exquisite."

"New."

He trailed his fingers over the satin cups of her bra.

"Nice." He released the front clasp and cupped her breasts in his large hands, watching in delight as her nipples beaded beneath his thumbs. "Exquisite."

She closed her eyes, tipping her head back against the door as he flicked the tip of his tongue over one nipple. Her hands searched blindly, finding his head and clutching it to her chest. She arched her back, offering him more of her breast.

He suckled deeply while easing her hair over her opposite shoulder. He backed away enough to admire the fall of her hair down one side of her body. With one nipple rosy and wet from his mouth, the other hidden, and ruffled red panties peeking at him from beneath the heavy fall of her hair, *his wife* stole his breath.

When she shifted nervously her right nipple poked between the strands of her hair. With a guttural groan he swooped in to take control of it, his focus shattering when her hands cupped the sides of his face and stroked tenderly. If he was going to have any chance of doing all the things he'd dreamed of, she needed to keep her hands to herself. When a plan stormed his brain, he ran with it.

"Come with me." He led her to the bathroom and closed the door, scowling at the lack of hooks on the back of it. The shower would have to do. Ignoring her questioning look, he backed her into the shower. He pushed her breasts together, admiring her exaggerated cleavage even as he teased her nipples with his thumbs.

She looked around wildly. "Wait! I've got heels on."

"No water. Trust me."

For a moment he thought she'd argue, but his mouth on hers seemed to win her over. He pulled back, gathering her hair into his hand at her nape then holding her gaze as he looped it over the shower head and tied a loose knot. Her eyes glazed with something close to alarm, her hands reaching upward in automatic response.

"Sh." He leaned in and tried to replicate the absolute sweetness of their first kiss, his hands covering hers on the shower head.

Her mouth responded to his, but the jerky movement of her hands told him she was conflicted. She shifted, moaning when her puckered nipples dragged across his lapels.

He thrust his chest forward, bending his knees a little to vary the stimulation. He trailed his lips across her cheek and spoke against her ear. "Just relax for me, Sara. Widen your feet a little for balance, close your eyes and hold on tight."

The moment her feet edged apart, he knew he had her. Slowly, one hand at a time, he released his hold on her. He stroked his fingers back and forth above her panties, maintaining contact as he took in the sight of her. His damn hand was shaking as he slid lower, the battle between urgency and awe raging out of control within him.

Her sudden intake of air steadied him. She was wildly out of her comfort zone, virtually naked, restrained by her hair, and teetering on skyscraper heels. For him.

He massaged her through her panties, stifling a groan as he realized how wet she was. When she pressed against his palm, he did groan. He tweaked one nipple sharply while softly lapping at the other, his hand moving lazily between her legs, soaking her panties with her juices.

Her breathing grew shallow, her entire body swaying as she clung to the shower head and allowed him to pleasure her. He dropped to a squat, guiding her legs together so he could peel her panties down. His heart damn near stopped when he spied a small foil packet in an ingenious hidden pocket beneath the red ruffles. He rattled the packet, grinning when she laughed breathlessly.

"It's for you."

His hands clawed at his clothing, settling for undoing his belt and dropping his pants and boxers. He tore the packet and rolled it on, positioning his cock at the entrance to her body and probing gently. "Look at me."

He held her gaze as he slowly slid inside her, watching for the moment this position would become awkward. "Put your hands on my shoulders. Slip one shoe off at a time." He didn't have to say anything else. She wanted to wrap her legs around him, and cling tight as he supported her gorgeous heart-shaped bottom. He filled her over and over, feeling her rising tension as she neared climax. He gritted his teeth, bouncing her slightly, willing her to hurry. "Come for me."

She did, instantly. He stilled, allowing her orgasm to send him over the edge. God he loved being married. Nothing could compare.

• • •

Sara tried to move her leg and found that it was weighted down. Three separate sets of memories bombarded her mind and she flushed a deeper red than last night's dress. Ethan hadn't been kidding when he'd said sleep was overrated.

She woke him gently, sliding her flattened palm across his stomach, shrieking in surprise when he captured her hand.

"Zoe got a room here as well. I told her we'd meet her for breakfast at nine, so we don't have time. Ethan!"

His hand began a slow descent, dragging hers with it.

"Stop that." She smiled at him, feeling tempted despite her promise to Zoe. "This isn't a choice between breakfast and bed. We don't have to checkout till midday."

She patted his shoulder when he grumbled.

"Take a few extra minutes to wrap your head around the idea." She slid out of bed and into a robe, casually twirling the belt. "I'll be in the shower. Alone. Naked." She laughed when he caught the end of her belt. He tugged and she let the robe slip off, making a dash for the bathroom, knowing he'd follow.

She'd half expected management to pound on the door and carry on about a fair use water policy, but her half hour shower with Ethan went unnoticed. She was running late for breakfast, and she still hadn't told Ethan about the appointment she'd made to look at office space, but those were minor concerns. Nothing could go wrong on a day that started this fabulously.

She tried not to skip as she rushed down the hall toward the café. Ethan was on the phone with his PA, so she'd left him behind. She rounded a corner and collided with a couple walking toward her.

"Sara?"

"Gabe?" Her gaze swung between her ex and the woman tucked against his side, a sick sense of dread rising within her. "What are you doing here?"

The woman, a compact blonde, answered for him. "We changed the destination of the return flights so we could catch up with my parents here in LA on our way home. Phuket was lovely, by the way." She giggled. "Everything you organized was perfect, even that silly old church. You should consider wedding planning as a fulltime career."

What the hell?

She stared at the woman's left hand, scarcely able to draw breath as the truth hit her. Gabe had chosen to marry this… person, instead of her.

"Sara?" Gabe's voice sounded weird, kind of far away and muffled. "Are you okay?"

She tried to focus, and couldn't.

"Sara! Are you okay?"

James' face appeared suddenly, seeming dangerously close to hers. Moments later she was leaning heavily against him, grateful for his support.

"Zoe sent me to look for you. And just in time, too." His tone hardened as he turned his attention away from her. "I'm guessing you're Gabe? I think you've done your worst. It's time you left."

Gabe had just started to argue when Ethan's voice cut him off.

"Get the hell away from my wife. What more could you possibly want from her? You've already wasted four years of her life. Then you stood her up at her dream wedding and married someone else, on Sara's dime." Ethan sliced his hand through the air. "She paid, you got the benefit, and the insurance policy is void because the event still went ahead."

Sara's body felt bruised all over, as if every new revelation was a physical blow. Gabe appeared to have acted reprehensibly, but Ethan's knowledge, his deception, tore her apart.

It was impossible not to trust a man who scraped your life up off the floor and helped reassemble it. When he, too, turned out to be a self-serving jerk, it was time to swear off men altogether.

"Sara?" Gabe's hand hovered above her forearm before dropping to his side. "I'm sorry. I broke it off with Jess before I met you, because our relationship didn't seem to be going anywhere. Your future plans looked so good, so definite, that I wanted to be part of them. I thought I'd fall for you, eventually." He shook his head. "It's always been Jess, Sara. I couldn't stop picturing her in your place at the wedding, so I called it off. Jess and I knew we had to cancel everything, but somehow we couldn't. The date got closer, and then you left, and it was all set up, ready to go... It might take a while, but we'll find a way to repay the money."

I don't care about the money.

She stared blankly at Gabe, willing him to go away. He was inconsequential compared to Ethan. Her hopes for a dream wedding had been massive. They'd defined her, setting her apart, making her special, and Gabe had been a big part of that. He'd worked alongside her, helping her to achieve her dreams.

Ethan, on the other hand, had assessed her problems from a distance. He'd devised a quick fix that involved lying and manipulating the situation to his own advantage. God, when she thought of the things he'd kept from her: Gabe's marriage and the fact that her insurance policy was void.

They weren't small deceptions.

If whisking her away to LA to live with him had seemed like a better option than telling her the truth, he must have a pretty low opinion of her coping skills. She would have been emotional if he'd levelled with her as soon as he found out about Gabe's marriage. She couldn't deny it, but she wouldn't have been heartbroken.

Now she wasn't so sure.

Chapter Fourteen

Back in their room, Ethan's concern for Sara grew. She'd withdrawn into herself, doing that oh-so-polite thing she'd done when she was hungover. Every time she nodded, agreed, or blindly accepted something, his tension ratcheted higher.

"Sara?" He hesitated, torn between comforting her until she recovered, or baiting her until she snapped at him. "It's almost midday. Do you want to head home or stay another day?"

"Home?"

Her flat, expressionless voice was the scariest thing he'd ever heard.

"You should go. I'll stay. Here's as good a place as any for me."

The walls of the small hotel room felt as if they were closing in. It wasn't in his nature to sit around and wait. Her ex and his next were here in LA. There'd never be a better time for her to slip back into her hometown in Utah and tie off any loose ends.

He paced to the far side of the room and called his PA at home.

"Find out if there's a direct flight to Salt Lake City from LAX this afternoon. Two. Yeah, myself and Sara." He stifled a grin when Sara sprang off the bed and stalked toward him. "Ah, Sara has something to add. Let me call you back."

"Don't handle me, Ethan. I'm not going back to Utah, and I want that divorce you promised me. I'm not blissfully happy, and you have no hope of changing that inside of two weeks. You've lost the bet. Pay up."

He studied her, wondering what had prompted her to ask for a divorce ahead of schedule. He'd begun to hope that their thirty-day marriage might stretch to sixty-days and then a hundred. No pressure, just a natural extension. Sharing his home with her was the biggest commitment he'd ever made, and it was something he was willing to build on. He smiled benignly and gathered their luggage before opening the door for her.

"After you. We're taking this discussion home."

Her loose hair bounced delightfully as she swanned past him.

"The home ground advantage won't help you that much."

"Of course not. It's your home too."

"Not for long. I don't intend to live with you while you process our divorce papers."

He was surprised she didn't continue their argument. Her silence in the car was unnatural, her tightly clasped hands hinting at inner turmoil. When they got home she went downstairs without a word.

"We missed breakfast, so I'm phoning in a lunch order."
His voice echoed off the walls of the stairwell. "I'll collect it
because it'll be quicker. What do you feel like?"

She didn't answer, so he took a guess. When he arrived
home an hour later, the house was empty and all of her pos-
sessions were gone.

Two weeks later, Sara moved out of her budget motel room
into the new apartment she'd rented. It looked amazing and
she couldn't wait to show Zoe. A stranger approached her as
she walked from her car to Zoe's front door.

"You are Sara Kate Greaves?" The guy waited for her
nod and then thrust what appeared to be an invitation into
her hands. "You are served."

She almost laughed. This was absurd. These weren't divorce papers, so what were they? And how did anyone know
where she'd be? She signed for the delivery and carefully
opened the envelope. Wow, there seemed to be about twenty
invites stacked one on top of the other. She shrugged and
read the uppermost invitation.

> *Sara, I miss you. I miss things I didn't even know
> existed before I met you. I admit I made some poor
> choices on your behalf, and compounded them by
> being secretive. They're decisions I can't take back,
> but I will never stop trying to win you over.*

> *Keeping everyone at a distance is my biggest weak-
> ness. I hate to reveal anything personal, and I use my
> job to justify my single status.*

So, in light of my numerous shortcomings, let me say this: I've fallen in love with you. I haven't perfected it yet, but I've adopted your way of catering for two with every decision I make. And if you'll let me, I'll gladly propose to you in public. And follow it up with the wedding of your choice. Our life together is yours to direct, because without you, I'm just a cynical man in an expensive suit.

Love always,
Ethan Munroe

P.S. You may distribute the remaining copies to anyone you choose. Yours is the only opinion that matters.

Sara's limp hands lost their grip on Ethan's stack of gilt-edge confessions.

"Litterbug."

Ethan's gentle reprimand sent her pulse rocketing skyward. She remained with her back to him, unsure what to do or say next. A few pretty words couldn't erase all that he'd done. If she forgave him, brushed aside the churning misery and regret of the past few weeks, it would be like admitting that she didn't really matter.

Zoe appeared at the top of the steps and Sara had an idea. She stooped down to pick up the stack of gilt-edge cards and glanced at Ethan.

"For Zoe?"

At his nod, she climbed half the stairs and held one out to Zoe. "This is for you. I'll call you later?"

"Sure. And Sara? Push for what you want. Don't settle for less, okay?"

"My dreams are less elaborate these days. I just want to be happy." She turned toward Ethan. He looked tired, stressed, and older. He also looked hopeful.

Sara tried to give him one of those stern lawyer-looks he did so well. "Words on paper? Is that all you've got?"

She'd meant it as a joke, but Ethan shook his head.

"No. I thought you might want this back." He handed her a small red box. "If you don't, you could always pawn it."

A big ass diamond ring from Tiffany had no place in her life with Ethan. For the moment she didn't want a ring at all, or a public declaration of love, or a proposal. She simply wanted Ethan's time. She wanted dawn surfing lessons, impromptu dinner parties, sparkling fundraisers, and another trip to Vegas. A lazy one where room service featured heavily and leaving their room was optional. She grinned and slipped into Ethan's arms.

"It's far too showy. There's a place in Vegas where I'm sure we could offload it."

His slow, sexy smile made her stomach flip. Clearly his thoughts weren't centered on the pawnshop either. "We'd probably have to stay for a while. Eat crepes, drink tequila, that sort of thing."

"No shots for me. I still remember what I felt like the next day." She stretched upward and pressed her lips to the dimple in his chin. "Crepes sound good, though. And I didn't make it to the pool at all last time." She played her lips over his then gave him a significant look. "I missed out on room service too."

He stilled, something close to reverence shining in his

eyes. "And is that something you want?"

"Yeah." She shared a smile with him. "But before we start planning too far ahead, I'd like to show you the apartment I rented downtown." She shook her head to discourage him from talking. "It's convenient for meeting with clients, and thanks to Zoe, you'd be surprised how many I have. You might be wondering what makes it worthy of your appreciation…"

"It's near my office, isn't it?"

"Close enough for you to stop by on your lunch break."

He checked his watch. "It's almost midday."

She nodded. "On day thirty of our marriage. Didn't you promise I'd be blissfully happy today? I believe you guaranteed it."

He slid her peasant top off both shoulders and tugged it dangerously low, feasting his eyes on the upper slopes of her breasts. "Trust me, you will be."

He dipped his head to her chest, seeming to have forgotten they were standing in the street. She stumbled backward, laughing and calculating how winded she'd be if she sprinted home from here. He wouldn't be expecting her to run. Chasing her probably wasn't part of his plan, but plans changed.

Acknowledgments

Many thanks to my lovely editor, Alethea.

About the Author

Robyn lives with her husband and two sons on the outskirts of Melbourne, one of the most livable cities in the world. Writing romance helps to balance the effects of living in an all-male household. She loves to cook, hates to clean up, and keeps very odd hours. She's almost certain that cheesecake is the sixth major food group.

Discover the **What Happens in Vegas** *series…*

TEMPTING HER BEST FRIEND

Tired of waiting for her best friend to see her as more, Alyssa Miller heads to Las Vegas for a romance book convention. But when Dillon Alexander realizes his best friend plans to have a one-night stand on her vacation, he hauls ass after her to make sure he's the one to scratch her itch—commitment issues be damned. Neither of them expects their chemistry to be so explosive, but with a little help, what happens in Vegas might not stay in Vegas…

THE MAKEOVER MISTAKE

Also by Robyn Thomas…

HIS UNEXPECTED FAMILY

FAMOUSLY ENGAGED